Forged in Fire, Stone and Steel

Forged in Fire, Stone and Steel

By R.B. Glynn

Dedication

For those who bore weights too great to carry, yet continued on all the same.

For those who endured silence and shackles, yet still dared to dream of flame

and freedom. This story belongs to you. May you remember always that a

single spark can set the world ablaze.

Prologue

The first explosions came just past midnight. Anya stirred, dreaming of leading her army like a legend of old, before the thunder of actual violence snapped her awake. The chamber door crashed inward, the clash of iron and splintered oak cutting through the silence of the High Tower like a blade through silk.

Valdek, the majordomo of House Velmira, stumbled through the doorway, blood running freely down his face from a cut above his eyebrow, catching in his neatly trimmed beard. Although a servant by title, none commanded as much respect within the castle as he did, not even the royal family.

"Branislav, ward it!" he quietly ordered over his shoulder.

A man in battle-worn armour stumbled in, a bloodied sword in one hand, his well-worn mace in the other. Even with the scratches and dirt from recent combat, his insignia was still proudly visible on his cuirass, marking him as the master of arms.

After glancing through the doorway to make sure no one followed them, he carefully placed his weapons on a side table and dragged the richly adorned wardrobe across the floor with unexpected strength from one so old. With a final shove, the old man jammed it against the shattered door just as another explosion rocked the stone walls. The sounds of footsteps and screams echoed from below.

Anya sat up, clutching the tangled silken sheets around her, blinking against the candlelight. Her dark hair hung loosely above her shoulders.

"What's-?"

"There's no time to explain. Put these on," the majordomo said, his voice calm but deadly serious, passing her a bundle of clothes containing her riding boots, pants and a thick woollen coat. "On your feet, *Tsarevna*, quickly now."

She obeyed, her heart pounding, as she pulled the cloak over her nightdress. The urgency in his voice removed the need for modesty. The air in the room had turned sharp with smoke and something stranger, acrid and metallic.

"Is that fire?" she asked, moving to the ledge.

"No, it's…" Branislav growled. "It's much worse."

She looked out. The spires of the royal complex were burning. This wasn't any normal fire, but flames that burned stone, casting ethereal shadows across the rest castle and the town below.

The blaze burned red, blue and a deep green which Anya hadn't seen before. It was smokeless and crept slowly across the stonework. Above it all, strange glowing symbols twisted in the sky, flickering like dying stars.

"Is that… magic?!"

Valdek pulled her back from the window, covering them with heavy curtains embroidered with the green and gold falcon of her family. "Away from the window for now, Tsarevna. Don't forget the straps on your boots this time."

"Alchemy and illusions," Branislav muttered. "The magisters want everyone to believe that they are magical."

Another explosion shook the tower. Somewhere far below, the sound of metal shrieking against stone as the main gate was torn from its hinges.

"Gods," Anya whispered. "I heard they didn't have the strength."

"They don't," Branislav spat. "They're making it seem like they do."

From his belt, he drew a small dagger with a large sapphire in the pommel and handed it to her. The blade was ceremonial, but still razor sharp.

"They've made everyone believe, *malyshka*. They told the people the monarchy hoarded real power, while they bottled lightning and fire in copper tubes and glass flasks." He sighed heavily. "Even we believed them."

The majordomo pulled the curtains aside and pushed open the window, revealing a treacherous ledge that snaked down the cliffside. An escape path carved centuries ago, barely wide enough for a single person. Far below, the dark waves churned around jagged rocks. But there, almost invisible in the darkness, a torch flickered on a concealed dock nestled at the cliff's base.

"The eastern slip," said the majordomo. "There's a boat waiting for you, Tsarevna. We have only one chance."

She turned to him.

"And mother and father?"

Valdek looked towards Branislav, their eyes meeting briefly, deciding who would be the one to tell her.

Branislav clasped her shoulder. "The *Tsar* and *Tsarina* chose to stay behind, so that you could live."

Anya involuntarily dropped the pack she was holding. Something in her chest cracked, a small cry escaping, as her world collapsed around her.

"I can't leave them," she whispered, suppressing a sob.

"I'm afraid you must, malyshka," Branislav said, "I know it hurts, but you're not a child anymore, not after tonight. We don't have a choice."

Behind them, the door shuddered. The wardrobe groaned under the blow. Sparks of crimson light shot through the gaps. The magisters were here. Branislav turned towards the blocked door, picking up his weapons from the table.

"Take her. I'll slow them down."

"No heroics," Valdek hissed.

Branislav grinned grimly. "Only delay."

As Anya stepped onto the ledge. The wind clawing at her cloak, she glanced back, taking one last look at her home, its towers ablaze with false magic, its halls filled with ghosts and lies.

"They don't need a throne," she murmured. "Just belief."

The majordomo steadied her hand on the rock.

"Then give them something better to believe in."

They began the descent into the darkness.

***

Four magister guards marched through the open doorway into the throne room, their boots striking the flagstones in perfect unison. The sound echoed off the towering pillars. Sharp and deliberate, it announced their presence long before they reached the dais. Their ornate longswords were still slick with fresh blood, droplets falling to the stone and smearing beneath their steps. The smell of iron hung in the air, mingled with the faint scent of burning oil from the wall sconces and the alchemy of the magisters.

Close behind them came three magisters. At their centre walked a figure in a robe of almost colourless fabric, such a pale blue that it seemed to drink the glow of the torches. With each step, the robe shifted, revealing brief flashes of a strange glint beneath. A faint metallic grind followed him, the subtle click with every movement.

"Tsar Sokol. Tsarina Milla," the pale-robed magister said, his voice smooth and unhurried, as though the presence of armed men and the blood on the floor were of no consequence. "How very noble, sitting here in the heart of your crumbling kingdom."

The guards spread out on either side, their gazes cold and unblinking. The two other magisters took positions slightly behind the central figure, their staves tilted at an angle, as though ready to strike at the slightest word.

The Tsar's jaw tightened. His hand curled around the carved armrest of his throne, the knuckles whitening. "You come armed into the royal hall and spill blood throughout my keep. Do you think this will go unchallenged? Do you think you can get away with this?"

The pale-robed magister tilted his head ever so slightly, as though weighing the Tsar's words like an academic curiosity. "Alas, we do what we must," he said at last, his voice carrying an unshakable finality. "And it is far beyond your understanding."

"I understand enough," the Tsar replied, his tone hardening. "You defy the crown, the order of the realms and the very laws that bind us. That will not be forgotten, nor forgiven."

A faint, almost pitying smile touched the magister's lips. "You cling to the law because you think it protects you. But the law serves those who have the will to enforce it." His voice lowered, and for the first time, there was an edge beneath the calm. "Now, tell me… where is your daughter?"

The question hung in the air like a drawn blade.

Tsarina Milla leaned forward on the arm of her throne, her eyes narrowing with defiance. "She is gone," she said, her voice full of pride. "Far from your reach."

The magister's head turned toward her slowly, the faint clicking underscoring his movement. "No one is beyond our reach, my dear," he murmured.

Suddenly, two magister guards stepped into the throne room. Between them, they dragged the limp, bloody form of Branislav, his head lolling forward, leaving a faint trail of red on the polished stone. His once-pristine gambeson was torn and soaked through, the deep gashes across his chest still glistening.

One magister, cloaked in a deep crimson robe embroidered with copper runes, broke away from the others. He moved with deliberate steps, the hem of his garment brushing against Branislav's legs as he crouched beside him. With clinical detachment, the magister pressed two fingers to the man's throat, feeling for the faint thrum of life.

"He still lives," the crimson-robed magister muttered with a sly smile.

The magister in the pale robe stepped forward. He stopped beside the crimson-robed figure, tilting his head slightly, the shadow of his hood hiding his expression. Leaning down, he whispered, his voice low but sharp enough to carry in the tense silence of the room.

"We will find a use for him. Good."

The final word stretched out, dripping with malice, promising that this was just the beginning

Chapter One

The forge had been burning since before first light, a low, humming roar beneath the peaks surrounding the Kul Vazhen valley. Smoke rose in ribbons from the chimney, vanishing into the cold air like unheard prayers to the many forgotten gods.

Inside the smithy, Daran worked the bellows while his father hammered at a glowing strip of ore, beads of sweat glinting in the firelight. The anvil rang with each strike, rhythmic and sharp, as he worked the metal, not just mere iron, but the mighty earthen steel. Metal infused with the valley's most sacred resource, essence drawn from the veins of the earth itself.

"You're slowing down on me, boy," his father grunted, without looking up.

Daran rolled his eyes and kept pumping. "The fire's already full. You'll melt the roof beams if I go any faster."

"Is that so?" His father glanced over his shoulder, a crooked grin breaking through the soot on his face. "Or are your arms tired from sneaking off to see that girl of yours again?"

Daran flushed. "I wasn't-"

"Oh sure. You just happened to go missing right as Ora was walking past the well yesterday, huh?" He gave the ingot a hard strike. "Betrothed or not, you keep slacking like this and she'll be the one swinging the hammer while you watch."

Daran snorted. "She'd probably do a better job."

"She probably would, at that," his father said with a chuckle, then fell quiet for a moment, just the sound of metal on metal filling the space. "You're lucky, Daran. Some people don't get to choose who they work beside. Or who they love."

Daran didn't reply. He just kept the bellows going, trying to ignore the tightness in his chest.

When the heat grew unbearable, his father finally waved him off. "Go get us some water."

Daran gladly escaped into the valley air, heading towards the well. Morning mist clung low between the ridges, and the musty smell of fallen leaves drifted in the breeze.

Ora was already there, her brown hair bound back in braids with a strip of red cloth, her sleeves were rolled up as she drew water. She spotted him instantly, her mouth breaking into a sly grin.

"You look exhausted," she teased as he approached, eyeing the soot that covered his dark skin. "Are you letting the forge get the better of you again?"

"It's better the heat of forge than that of my father," Daran muttered, lowering his voice as he leaned close. "He thinks I disappear every time you walk past."

Her laugh rang softly but bright, like the strike of a small bell. "Well, he's not wrong." She pressed the bucket handle into his hands. "While you're here, you can carry this."

He grumbled, but took it anyway. "You just want an excuse to boss me around."

"You'd fall apart without me, and you know it." She bumped her shoulder lightly against his, then sobered a little. "How bad will it be this year?"

Daran swallowed, looking toward the high road. "Bad. Father says we're still a few ingots short..."

Her smile faded. She reached to touch his arm, her fingers leaving faint damp prints on the soot. "Just...stay quiet when they come. Don't give them any reason."

He nodded, forcing a smile he didn't feel.

By the time he returned to the forge, the spirit of the valley had shifted. The clang of metal carried sharper in the thin air, and tension coiled through the streets. Even the mountain wind seemed to hold its breath.

***

"They'll be here by midday," his father added after a moment, his tone shifting. "And we're still short three ingots."

Daran's smile faded. He pumped harder, jaw clenched.

The magisters' tax started fifteen years ago and every year without fail, the heavily armed convoy came from the capital, winding down the only road through the Ironjaw Gate and its treacherous pathways until it finally reached Kul Vazhen. They took ore and essence from every mine and metals from every forge.

Outside, hooves clattered on stone. A horn sounded, shrill and triumphant.

"They're early," Daran hissed.

His father swore under his breath, tossing the half-finished bar aside. He wiped his hands on his apron, as if to clean them, but they remained dirty. "Stay quiet. Let me talk."

Two magisters guard strode in with red-and-gold cloaks and gleaming breastplates with the subtle richness of tourmaline. They were covered in earthen steel. But there was no nobility in their gaze, only disdain for the lesser folk. They were followed by a sneering middle-aged magister with a silver-threaded sash, which denoted his rank of chancellor. He dismounted and strode into the smithy like it belonged to him.

"You're late, Boran," he said, knowing full well that they weren't.

"We've nearly met the weight," Daran's father said, bowing. "Three more ingots an-"

"*Nearly!*" the magister cut in, eyes narrowing. "Nearly doesn't keep the army supplied. Nearly doesn't show your dedication to the Protectorate!"

He turned to his men. "Make him an example."

They grabbed Boran and shoved him hard against the anvil. He grunted, his hands outstretched in protest.

"Please," he gasped. "Another hour... just one—"

A fist drove into his stomach sharply, stealing his breath. Then another. This time harder, folded him forward.

The guard with a large scar down his jaw grabbed Boran's tunic and tore it open, exposing his ebon chest to the heat of the forge and the icy mountain air. The other cracked the pommel of his sword down across Boran's back, sending a jolt of pain through his spine and dropping him to one knee. His father grunted beneath their boots, still pleading, trying to shield his face.

Daran stood frozen. His chest heaved and his fists trembled.
His eyes darted to the tool rack by the anvil.

The hammer.

His hammer.

The one he'd shaped through long nights last winter under the scrutiny of his
father. Its haft worn smooth by his own hands. It wasn't a weapon, but a tool.
But it was strong and heavy.

He didn't think. He just moved.

With a roar, Daran lunged forward and seized the hammer from the rack.

Before the nearest guard could turn, Daran swung. A full-body arc of fury
and struck him at the shoulder.

The sound was dull and final.
The man crumpled, screaming, his shoulder a ruin of bent metal and shattered
bone.
Earthen steel, for all its vaunted strength, had no mercy for its own kind. When
matched against itself, it came down to weight, speed and will.

The second guard turned, eyes wide.
Daran swung again, but his rage made him wild, the hammer flew past the
man's head, missing by inches.

The third blow never came.

A mailed fist crashed into the side of his skull. Then another. Knuckles like boulders slammed into his temple.

Then…nothing.

The darkness swallowed him.

***

He woke in chains. The stones beneath his cheek were just as cold and unforgiving as the steel that bound him.

The distant voices echoed off the walls of the square.

Daran stirred, groaning. Every movement sent pain lancing through his ribs and skull.

His wrists were shackled in earthen steel, the silver-grey metal with that faint, telltale brown shimmer that caught the morning light like smouldering coals.

It was his father's work.

He could tell by the tightness of the links, the clean edge of the clasps. They were strong enough to hold a bull, and more than strong enough to hold him.

He blinked against the blur, his vision swimming into focus.

They had gathered everyone in the village.

Villagers knelt or sat in lines across the square. Miners, masons, smelters, haulers, and their families. Some were bleeding, while others simply stood silently, too scared to speak.

Children clutched their mothers' sides. Old men stared with empty eyes, a knowing look of what was to come.

A few of the younger workers still looked ready to fight, but they were beaten and bound, their tools confiscated, and the guards standing over them carried blades, cudgels and arrogance in equal measure.

A young woman was loudly arguing with one guard, pushing him away from her despite her bound hands.

The air stank of smoke, sweat, and fear. The forge fires had been snuffed out. Overturned were the anvils, and the millstones halted. The magisters had brought silence to Kul Vazhen valley, and silence here was never a good thing.

Near the fountain at the square's centre, the magister stood atop a stack of crates. His crimson cloak snapped in the breeze, the silver sunburst of the Protectorate gleaming on his back. His voice, oily with sneer yet deliberate and cutting, carried across the square.

"Those who are strong will serve. Those who are weak will be crushed. The Protectorate has no use for those who cannot pay their due."

His words rippled through the square like a chill wind.

Daran's fists tightened, the earthen steel digging into his skin.

He turned his head and saw his father a few paces away, slumped to one knee, blood on his brow, both hands bound behind his back with the same chains he had crafted with pride.

A flicker of shame passed over Daran like a shadow. This was his fault. This was because he had snuck away with Ora when he should have been working. There was no justice in this, this wasn't the tax they had been promised. This was a message, and they were the parchment it would be written on.

The magister's words hung heavy in the bitter air, an unusual stillness foreign to the town.

But a sudden, sharp voice cut through the silence.

"This is wrong!"

Daran's breath caught as he turned his head. There, near the edge of the crowd, stood Ora, her dark eyes blazing with fury, fists clenched at her sides.

"This is our home, our lives! Even when we have nothing left to give, you would take even that?!"

Her voice trembled, raw with desperation and courage.

One of the magister guards stepped forward, lips curling into a cruel smile.

Before anyone could react, his hand shot out, backhanding Ora across the face with a sickening smack.

"Silence, wench."

She staggered backwards, her braids whipping to the side, a sharp gasp escaping her lips as blood bloomed on her cheek.

A murmur rippled through the villagers. Shock, fear, and outrage.

Daran's chains bit deeper into his wrists as his muscles surged with fury and helplessness. He struggled violently against the earthen steel cuffs. Gritting his teeth, he pushed himself to his feet.

"Leave her alone!" he roared, his voice ragged.

The guards turned toward him and advanced, clubs raised without hesitation.

Blows rained down on Daran's shoulders, back, and head, each strike sapping what little strength he had left.

He collapsed to the cold, hard ground. His breath wheezed as pain flared like coals beneath his skin.

Ora, though blood ran from her mouth, remained on her feet.

Her eyes, fierce and unyielding, scanned the crowd.

"We must fight back!" she cried, voice breaking but determined. "We are stronger than their chains! The magi do not own us! For your homes, your families and your lives!"

For a moment, the villagers stirred, a flicker of hope, a whisper of defiance.

"Silence her. Now." The magister snapped towards one of his guards.

Before the villagers could act, the guard moved fast and deliberate. His blade gleamed in the morning sun as it plunged through Ora's back.

She screamed, a sound of pure agony and shattered hope, and crumpled to the ground, clutching the wound.

The crowd froze, terror flooding their faces. Daran's spirit shattered with her as she fell.

His breath caught in his throat as Ora collapsed. Dark blood seeped through her fingers and pooled in the cracked stone.

He struggled to rise, to reach her, but the chains held firm. They bit into his wrists and dragged him back down.

His fists slammed against the unforgiving metal, desperation fuelling every blow.

"Ora!" he gasped, voice raw and breaking.

The crowd pulled away from her, paralysed by fear and pain. The rebellion that had briefly flickered in their eyes was snuffed out, replaced by silent submission.

The magister guard closed ranks around their charge, weapons raised towards the villagers, their eyes cold and watchful.

The magister descended from his makeshift platform. His expression unreadable but merciless.

He surveyed the scene, then nodded once.

The guards began hauling the bound villagers toward the waiting carts and wagons, their chains clinked like a death knell throughout the valley.

Daran's gaze lingered on Ora's face, the fight extinguished from her eyes even as she clung to life.

***

The wind howled down from the mountainous heights, whispering through the broken windows and scorched eaves of Kul Vazhen. Smoke curled from half-burned homes. No laughter, no hammer-song. Just boots and chains.

Daran stood slumped in the line of villagers, his hands bound behind him. Each link felt heavier than the one before it. His whole body ached. His thoughts drifted back to Ora's scream, that terrible sound still echoed in his chest.

He glanced sideways and saw her blood still drying on the stones.

A nudge broke his haze. A thick, familiar shoulder brushed against his. His father now stood next to him, his chin bruised, and his lips cracked, but his eyes remained as steady as ever.

"Boy…" Boran murmured, his voice like gravel over steel. "You still with me, boy?"

Daran nodded, swallowing the lump in his throat. "It's all my fault…"

"It's not your fault, son." He paused. "The magisters are monsters."

Daran looked away. "If I hadn't gone to see Ora and had kept working the forge…"

Boran huffed. "That wouldn't have changed anything. They wanted to send a message to all of Rosk."

They stood together in the dust, chained and silent for a moment. Around them, guards barked orders as they finished dragging the last of the prisoners and supplies toward the carts lined up at the edge of the square.

"Where is Ora?" Daran finally asked, his voice nearly breaking.

Boran's jaw tensed. He didn't answer immediately.
"She's gone, son."

The words hit harder than any hammer could. Daran bowed his head, biting his tongue to keep from screaming.

One of the magister guards passed by and glared at them. "No talking," he snapped, jabbing Boran's shoulder with the tip of his sword. Boran grunted, but didn't respond.

They were shoved forward in a shuffling line, their chains rattled with every step. Once they reached the carts, more open wagons with tall iron rails along the outside, and in the middle, they were herded inside like cattle. The floor was straw and splinters. Daran stumbled upwards, catching himself against his father's side.

The villagers were packed tightly, seated shoulder to shoulder. Some wept quietly, others stared blankly ahead, their minds already far from this place.

As the last few prisoners were loaded, the magister mounted his horse, seated tall with his face hidden beneath his hood. His voice rang out once more.

"The taxes have been collected. The strong conscripted. Kul Vazhen has served the Protectorate."

He turned his horse without another word.

The convoy began to move. Hooves pounded the earth, wheels creaked. The village faded behind them, the forge, the temple, the cliffside homes, all growing smaller with each jolt of the cart.

Daran didn't look back.

Beside him, Boran shifted and leaned across the cart, speaking low. "When the time comes," he whispered, "you don't stay broken. You hear me?"

Daran said nothing. His heart felt empty, but his father's words echoed within the hollowed chambers.

Chapter Two

The clang of steel echoed through the pine-clad hills.

Blades struck and sparked, feet shifted in mud, and steam rose from sweat-darkened tunics as two young men circled each other in the clearing. The chieftain's son, Tareq, was lean and quick, with long auburn hair pulled into a tight ponytail. The other, Nabil, tall and broad, with a cut already bleeding across his arm.

"You're dropping your shoulder again," barked a voice from the edge of the ring.

Banu, a grizzled warrior with a nose that had been broken too many times, spat into the dirt. "The magi's guards will see that feint coming a mile away."

Tareq grinned, his sword angled high. "Only if he lives that long."

He lunged, the rhythm of his boots matching the beating war-drums he'd grown up hearing through the camp. His opponent parried well, but Tareq twisted, sliding the flat of his blade down his opponent's sword and into the cross guard and rammed his shoulder forward, throwing him off-balance. The larger man staggered. In a flash, the chieftain's son sliced downwards and knocked the sword from his friend's hand.

"Yield?"

The boy scowled, then grunted, raising his hands in surrender. "Yield."

Cheers and hoots rang out from the watching Stags, men and women dressed in a weathered assortment of leathers and furs, scarred by wind and steel. Each bearing the mark of the Flying Stag. They had antlers with wings carved into pendants or tattooed on what visible skin they had. Their camp was never still for long. Tents woven from elk hide, carts heavy with what little they owned, children darting between the fires playing with wooden swords.

Their chieftain, Jahlan Sword-Hand, stood at the edge of the crowd, arms crossed, his cloak of winter lion fur stirring in the mountain wind. He nodded once, then called out:

"That was clean, Tareq. But clean cuts don't matter if you're too slow to swing."

Tareq lowered his blade and bowed his head, more from tradition than humility.

"You drill hard," Jahlan said, softer now as he stepped closer, "but you must learn to fight with more than pride. Every strike you make carries the weight of your people. Never forget that."

Jahlan continued. "With that excitement over, we move to serious matters. Tomorrow, we ride for the Fenline Gorge. The magi are moving supplies west, and they think our hills are quiet and safe. We're going to show them just how wrong they are."

The crowd cheered and whooped with anticipation. Raids were how the Flying Stags lived, not out of cruelty, but necessity. Their people had no land to call home, not since the Protectorate burned the last of the western freeholds. They hunted, they scouted, they struck, and then they vanished.

"The scouts say they carry more than grain and iron this time," Jahlan said grimly. "Prisoners. Chained and branded."

Silence fell among them.

Tareq's jaw tightened. "We'll free them?"

Jahlan nodded. "We will. It doesn't matter how many guards the magi have with them. We will free them."

He raised a horn carved from mammoth tusk and let out a long, bellowing cry.

The rest of the tribe joined in, blades raised. Tareq felt it in his chest, that old rhythm, older than kings, older than crowns.

Tonight, they'd feast on smoked meat and cloudberry mead.

Tomorrow, they'd ride. Tomorrow, they'd fight.

***

The moon hung low over the Fenline Gorge, veiled in cloud, casting the world in shifting shades.

Tareq sat still in the branches of a wind-swept pine, a hand on the hilt of one of the curved swords at his hip, the other pressed against the mossy bark. Tareq preferred his kilij for this type of fight. His father always said the kilij was made for reckless fighters like him. They were fast, sharp, and unforgiving.

Ahead, Tareq could see torches flickering through the narrow pass. The caravan was coming. The magister's banners fluttered in the breeze; their silken threads were stained with rain.

He glanced at Nabil beside him, his face smudged with soot. The younger man's leg bounced nervously. "I count twelve guards, two magi," he whispered. "Four guards mounted, both magi. They have bottles and tubes in a belt across their chest."

"Essence Bombs," Tareq muttered. "Fire and air, most likely."

"Should I be worried?"

Tareq grinned widely. "Only if they see you."

The caravan ground to a halt in front of a lone man standing in the middle of the road, a sword in one hand, and a blade where his other forearm would be on the other.

A signal cry rose from the opposite ridge, three notes on a bone whistle, sharp and cold.

Now.

Tareq rolled down the branches, whistled back, and sprang down the slope like a mountain cat, drawing his blades. Behind him, thirty Stags moved in unison, blades drawn, faces darkened with soot or wrapped in wool and leather. No banners flew, and no mercy was given.

The magisters never saw them coming.

The lead wagon exploded into chaos as a burning pitch-pot arced from the ridge and shattered across its wheels, sending the horses into a frenzy. Tareq hit the trail with a bone-jarring thud, slashing low at the nearest guard's legs before he could draw his sword.

Shouts erupted from the guards as they realised the trap.

Arrows rained from the cliffs. One rider fell sideways, twitching, a shaft jutting from the gap in his armour at his neck.

The older magister raised his hand, his veins glowing bright blue with water essence. He shot his hand forward. "Aqueis!"

A geyser of water leaped from his hand like a javelin at the nearest group of fighters. One of the Stags was thrown backwards into a tree, a hole punched cleanly through his chest.

Tareq didn't falter. He darted through the mist, sliding beneath a swinging blade, and brought his curved blade up into the gap at the man's armpit, winding it outwards to thrust deeply into the man's chest. Blood sprayed across the dirt road.

A horn blast split the air, not as a signal, but as a challenge.

He looked up.

***

Jahlan's gaze cut through the curling smoke and steam. The guard captain emerged. Massive and deliberate, every step echoing like a hammer on stone. His armour gleamed as if untouched by battle, yet it did nothing to conceal the lethal precision radiating from him.

In his hands, a wide, two-handed sword shimmered faintly with distilled essence, not magic, but deadly enough that Jahlan felt its promise of violence before a strike was even made. The captain's eyes scanned the square, cold and calculating, and for a heartbeat, Jahlan understood that this was a predator who had never missed his prey.

The two men squared off.

"You've no claim here," the guard said calmly, his eyes boring into his ambusher. "Back away, and your men may leave with their lives."

Jahlan grinned, and took a guard with his sword low, and blade arm high.

They clashed.

The first exchange was brutal. Jahlan was fast, but the guard's technique was surgical. He drove forward, blade sweeping in wide arcs, ending in thrusts or feints. Jahlan ducked, pivoted, countered with his sword and swept with his blade-arm, the gleaming sword slicing in vicious arcs. Sparks flew. Blood sprayed.

Neither fighter faltered. With every blow Jahlan landed, the guard returned with interest.

A brutal downward cut slammed against Jahlan's shoulder. He staggered. Snarling, he stepped back, and with a practiced flourish, sheathed both blades.

The captain paused.

Jahlan drew again, fire leapt from the blades, igniting the air with a hiss of oil and flint. The forge-work channels in the scabbards had done their work.

A dozen Stags whooped from the trees nearby, rallying.

The captain didn't flinch. "Petty tricks."

"You would know". He replied with a wide grin, despite the pain.

The two men met again in a fury of flame and steel. Jahlan spun, slashed, drove the flaming blade-arm into the guard's pauldron, but the armour held. He roared, fire trailing from his sword in sweeping arcs, until the guard caught his sword arm at the wrist.

Jahlan growled, trying to stab with his blade-arm, but the guard headbutted him, then drove a knee into his stomach as he dropped him to the ground.

The fire sputtered as the sword fell to the snow.

The final blow came in silence. Jahlan collapsed in the mud, blood pouring from neck.

"Tareq, no!"

The young warrior stood frozen twenty paces away. His stomach churned. He looked down at his bloodied blade, then charged.

"For the Stags!"

The guard turned just as Tareq lunged.

Steel met steel.

But Tareq wasn't ready.

The guard sidestepped, grabbed his arm, and with one fluid motion, bent his arm backwards and slammed him face-first into the earth. The world flashed white.

The last thing he saw was Jahlan's fire guttering in the dirt.

***

Pain throbbed behind Tareq's eyes like the beat of the war drums he was so familiar with. Slowly, the haze of unconsciousness lifted.

Cold metal bit into his wrists. The sharp smells of sweat, dirt, smoke and blood filled his nose.

He blinked against the dim light of dawn just reaching over the tops of the mountains. His wrists ached with the weight of the chains. His father's fallen image still burned in his vision. He wanted to scream, but all that came out was a croak.

Around him, a handful of prisoners stirred. Bruised miners, weary farmers, several Stags too.

No words were spoken. Only the soft rattle of chains and muffled coughs.

Tareq tried to move, but the shackles held firm, and a searing pain shot up his arm.

He forced himself to take slow breaths.

A figure stirred beside him, a man with large gnarled hands, dark skin and dull but steady eyes.

"Where…?" Tareq croaked.

The man's lips moved slowly. "Captives. Just like the rest of us."

Tareq's gaze drifted toward the other prisoners.

"What happened… with the raid? Did my father…"

Boran's jaw tightened. He didn't meet Tareq's eyes at first.

His voice was low, so as to not draw the attention of the guards.

"I'm sorry, lad. If you're meaning the man with the flamin' swords, he fought like a storm, but there's nothing the likes of us can do against the magi."

The silence stretched between them, heavy as iron chains.

"Where are they taking us?" Tareq's voice was barely more than a whisper.

"I don't know," Boran said. His eyes narrowed, scanning the horizon. "We've been moving north… then west."

Tareq's stomach lurched. "West? That means… the Blackhold."

The name landed like a hammer. Every head in the cart snapped toward the young bandit.

Tareq's mind raced, images of whispered stories clawing at his thoughts. Endless experiments. Prisoners twisted by magisters' cruel experiments. Faces half-forgotten, reshaped into something inhuman.

"They use essence… to break people," he murmured, throat tight. "To reshape them."

Boran's jaw hardened. "It's no myth."

A shudder ran through the cart, chains clinking like distant bells of doom. Tareq's fingers clenched the edge of the wooden seat until his knuckles whitened. His breath came shallow, uneven. The weight of their fate settled in his gut, cold and immovable, like stone.

Chapter Three

The wheels of the prison cart groaned as it rolled out from the cover of trees, the forest thinned into what remained of a once prosperous farmland.

Ash and smoke hung heavy in the air, though no fires burned here now. Crops lay in ruined rows, trampled flat or left to rot. Blackened beams jutted from the remains of homes, skeletal and scorched, stripped of life.

Daran stared in stunned silence, his hands raw from the cuffs, his jaw tight. He'd never seen this far beyond his valley. He'd never imagined how far the magisters' shadow had spread, and the destruction they would cause.

Opposite him, an auburn-haired boy, close to his own age, watched the passing ruins with clenched jaw and hollow eyes.

Boran shifted, chains clinking as he tried to find a more comfortable position on the splintered bench. "You two can't be more than a year apart," he said, voice gentle. "Better to make friends now than wait for the pit."

Tareq glanced at Daran, his brow furrowed. "I'm Tareq," he said after a moment. "From the Western Freeholds, warrior of the Flying Stags."

Daran didn't look up. His eyes stayed fixed on the floorboards. Dirt crusted the cuffs of his trousers. His wrists were scraped raw.

Tareq hesitated. "Raided the magi convoy. Got caught."

Boran gave his son a quiet look, but didn't push him further.

Tareq tried again, softer this time. "What about you? Where're you from?"

Daran's voice was hoarse when it finally came. "Kul Vezhen."

Tareq blinked. "Kul Vezhen? I thought no one could touch that place."

Daran just shrugged.

"What happened?" Tareq asked.

Daran's shoulders tensed, the pain still clear in his eyes.

Boran stepped in gently. "The magi came early to collect their tax. They demanded more than we had. My boy tried to stop them."

Tareq looked between the two, understanding dawning in his expression. "They punished the entire village?"

Daran's jaw tightened, but still he said nothing. His silence now felt more brittle, strained.

"Bastards," Tareq muttered.

They rode on in silence for a while. The cart hit a rut, and their chains rattled.

Tareq finally leaned back, folding his arms. "Well, maybe we'll get another shot at them. One day."

Boran gave him a tired smile. Daran didn't look up.

But his left hand, bound as it was, had curled ever so slightly into a fist.

***

By the third day since the Stag's raid, the sky had turned to a smudge of grey. The land they crossed was dead. Not simply fallow but ruined. Trees were reduced to twisted stumps, the rivers ran dry.

As the caravan crested a ridge, the outpost came into view.

A stone palisade ringed a cracked courtyard, its gate made from scavenged beams and old iron. Inside, a handful of low buildings squatted around a small stone tower that rose from the centre. A magister relay tower, humming faintly with stored essence. Telltale coils of copper and ash-glass shimmered near its base.

The cart jerked to a halt just outside the gates. The magister guards barked orders to the prisoners to disembark, and their chains clanked as they obeyed.

Daran stumbled as he stepped down, boots crunching against broken gravel. He winced and leaned on Boran briefly, then caught himself and stood straight. Tareq followed close behind, scanning the walls. Watchmen stood above with spears and slingshot rifles slung over their backs.

"Keep your eyes down," one guard snapped, cuffing a boy who dared look around. "Anyone who tries to run becomes target practice."

Inside, the outpost was alive with activity. More prisoners were being herded from other carts, some from mountain mines, others with their heads shaved and backs scarred from past defiance. A fresh batch of guards waited at the supply depot, checking manifests and loading crates filled with grain, tools, and something that shimmered with a dull silver-blue that could only be elemental essence.

Daran's eyes lingered on them.

"They're restocking," Boran muttered. "Means it's still a few days to the Blackhold."

"The Blackhold," Tareq repeated, the name sharp on his tongue.

Daran turned to him then, only really seeing him for the first time. "You've heard of it?"

"Only campfire stories," Tareq said. "Worse than death. They say the magi strip you down, all the way down to your spirit, just to see how you work."

Boran hissed, "That's enough."

But it was too late. The words had sunk in. Around them, several of the other prisoners had gone quiet, eyes shifting toward the tower.

Two magisters crossed the yard, robes brushing the dust. Their voices were low but clear enough for the prisoners nearby to hear.

"...the last convoy brought barely a third of what was promised. If the vein in Kul Vazhen is drying, the breach won't hold."

"It will hold," the other replied curtly. "So long as the forges keep yielding earthen steel. We have enough for a season yet... maybe two. More if the tax is pressed harder."

"And if it isn't enough?"

A pause, then a faint smile. "Then the Protectorate will have no choice but to strip every mine south of the Ironjaw. The breach must be held..."

They moved on, the echo of their footsteps swallowed by the courtyard noise, but the weight of their words lingered like a storm brewing on the horizon.

A magister appeared atop the stone steps, clad in faded crimson robes lined with stained copper thread. His hands glowed faintly, rings on each finger pulsing in rhythm. He spoke with a voice sharpened by training and arrogance.

"Those destined for the Blackhold... you will not return."

The prisoner nearest the gate panicked, either from Tareq's words or the magisters. Pulling away, he ran towards the opening. The magister extended his arm towards him and shouted, "Ignium!" Flames shot from his fingers, engulfing the escaping prisoner.

He gave an animalistic smile, turned, and walked away.

A few prisoners were pulled from the crowd, the old, the sick and the slow. They were led towards the tower door.

The rest were chained together again and shoved back into the carts. New guards took the reins. Their uniforms clean and pressed, sterner looks in their eyes.

As the gates opened and the caravan continued west, the air seemed colder, heavier.

No one spoke for a long time.

Not Boran, or even Tareq.

By the time the Blackhold came into view, even the guards had gone silent.

The fortress didn't rise from the land. It clawed its way out of the sea. A jagged monolith of black stone, carved into the spine of a sheer-sided island just off the western coast. Waves crashed violently against the cliffs below, sending up spray that caught the dying light like ash and blood.

There were no docks. No welcome. Only a narrow bridge of stone, crumbling and slick with sea mist, connected the mainland to the island's single gate.

"Is that it?" Tareq asked quietly, his voice tight.

Boran nodded. "Aye. The Blackhold."

Daran squinted through the mist. The bridge looked barely wide enough for the cart. On either side was a large drop into swirling currents and jagged rocks. The air stank of brine, oil, and something older and deeper. Rot and rust, salt and old blood.

The convoy halted. They were at the final checkpoint.

A magister outpost marked the edge of the land, a squat building built on the cliffside, its beacon crackling with blue elemental fire. From there, a series of runed pylons lit the narrow bridge ahead.

Daran shifted his weight, his chains clinking. "We're really going out there?"

"And there's no coming back," Boran muttered, voice low. "I'm sorry, lad."

Beyond the bridge, the fortress loomed. Four massive towers, each positioned at a corner of the island, with long, narrow walls connecting them like a monstrous crown. There were no visible windows. No signs of life.

A signal flare burst from a tower. Moments later, the magisters gave the order to move.

They crossed the bridge two carts at a time, flanked by armoured guards on foot. Every step sent a tremor through the wooden wheels, and the ocean screamed beneath them like it hungered for the fallen.

Daran didn't look down.

Tareq did.

"There are bodies in the water," he said. "By the gods… they don't even bury them."

"Burial's a mercy," Boran said through clenched teeth. "And there's no mercy here."

The gates of the Blackhold opened not with hinges, but by sliding silently into the mountain itself. Machinery groaned deep within the stone. Cold blue light danced across the gatehouse as the convoy rolled inside.

Darkness swallowed them, so did the heat.

Not the warmth of a hearth, but the stifling breath of industry, burning oil, molten slag and too many bodies pressed in a confined space. Deeper still came the sound of machines, hammering, grinding, screaming, alongside the unmistakable clatter of chains.

Inside, the fortress split into different levels. Ramps, pulleys, and lifts were carved into the rock. The prisoners were herded off the carts and sorted. Smiths, miners, scribes, healers, and… the rest.

"Seventy-two arrivals, only lost a handful along the way," a pale-robed magister confirmed, marking her ledger, her blonde hair pulled into a tight bun. "Begin the division. The strong to the forges. The weak to processing. The rest to Cell Block Seven."

The chain split. The three of them were pulled aside, along with five others from further down line. They were wiry, battered men and women in ragged furs beneath their chains. Warriors.

Tareq's people.

The other Flying Stags.

A guard shoved them forward with a grunt. "Special intake. Block Seven."

One of the older Stags scoffed through broken teeth. "Why not hang us with the rest? Get it over with."

The guard said nothing, just tightened his grip.

They were marched away from the main prison thoroughfare, deeper into the stone belly of the Blackhold. There were no torches here, just cold, flickering runes set into the walls, which provided light without warmth.

***

They passed sealed doors thick with sigils. Somewhere behind one, a woman screamed, high and thin. No one flinched. Not anymore.

Eventually, they reached a reinforced archway. No lock or latch, just a deep-scorched mark on the wall:

VII

The runes shimmered as a robed magister whispered something in a tongue Daran didn't recognize. The stone parted like melting wax.

Beyond was a wide, circular antechamber, ringed with iron and glass cells embedded in the walls like honeycombs. Each cage glinted with enchantments, not just to keep prisoners in.

Inside, a dozen already waited. Some lay slumped, bruised and thin. One stared at nothing. A girl in the far cell muttered softly in a loop, as though reciting instructions she didn't understand.

"This isn't a forge," one of the Stags muttered.

"No," Boran said grimly. "It's worse."

A magister emerged from the shadows, pale blue robes that flowed all the way to the ground. Long fingers, and eyes like burnished glass. A faint, quick clicking noise could be heard as he moved.

"Welcome to Block Seven. I am Fleshwright Ildran," he said smoothly. "You have been chosen not for what you are, but for what you might become. Fighters, craftsmen, dissidents. You are raw material with potential."

He stepped closer to Tareq. "Your band of Stags... interesting men. Difficult to kill. Even more difficult to predict."

Then to Boran, Daran and the others from the south, "And you, the last to forge earthen steel before the gates of Kul Vezhen fell."

Daran clenched his jaw.

The magister's voice never rose. "You will be tested, examined... measured. If you are strong, you will endure. If not..." A small smile. "We will find other uses for you."

They were ushered into shared cells, three or four per unit. Tareq, Boran, and two of the Flying Stags were placed together in a mid-tier cell, one bunk too few, iron benches, and a slop bucket. Daran was roughly shoved into a cell with two severely malnourished women.

The walls thrummed faintly with elemental charge.

As the door slammed behind them, a boy in the neighbouring cage, maybe ten years old. He was pale and twitching, with bandages all over his body, looked up. His voice was almost a whisper.

"They're watching, they're always watching. They want to see what you do. To see who you blame first."

Boran whispered to Daran through the bars. "Stay focused, boy," he murmured. "We'll find a way."

But Daran sat in silence, staring at the chains around his wrists

***

From the arched gate, the Fleshwright emerged. His pale blue robes trailed along the stones, somehow still pristine despite the surrounding filth. As he moved, a faint clinking accompanied each step, soft but precise, like glass tapping metal. It came from beneath the robes, where something unseen shifted with his movements.

The magister came to a halt before the cells where the new prisoners were put.

His face was bloodless, lips almost blue, eyes so pale they seemed almost white in the dim light. He studied the prisoners without expression, his hands folded behind his back beneath his flowing sleeves.

When his eyes fell upon Boran, he stopped.

Something about the man made him look again. Older, sturdier than the rest, with a smith's shoulders and a stillness rarely seen in prisoners.

Then the magister's gaze dropped.

A leather thong hung around Boran's neck, mostly concealed by the frayed edge of his collar. At the end of it: a flattened coin, worn to a soft gleam. The magister's eyes narrowed.

"Remove it," he said, voice like cooled steel.

A guard stepped forward, yanked the necklace free, and held it up.

The magister turned the coin over in his gloved fingers. A whisper of movement beneath the robes betrayed the faintest chime again. After a moment, he looked at Boran, this time with a flicker of curiosity.

"You wear the mark of the Earthen Hammer."

Boran said nothing.

"Separate him," the magister ordered. "Take him to the forges. Keep his hands unbroken."

Boran cast one last glance toward Daran. His son stood frozen in his cell, eyes wide with helplessness. The weight of his father's steady gaze, the memory of the hammer swinging in the forge, pressed heavily in Daran's chest.

Boran squared his shoulders as the guards pulled him away.

The magister drifted back toward the archway, robes whispering along the ground. With each step, the faint clinking continued, steady and rhythmic, like a spear tapping stone.

Chapter Four

Fifteen years ago, she had climbed out of her bedroom window in the dead of night, her silk nightgown torn by stone, royal slippers lost to the river's teeth.

Now, Anya stood at the head of a wind-blasted ridge, bow slung across her back, sword at her hip, and her eyes sharpened through hardship.

The young girl was gone.

What remained had been carved in ice and fury.

Below her, nestled in a gulch between the northern teeth of the Gorvani Range, the rebel camp stirred with life. Smoke curled from rough chimneys. Horses fussed and pawed at the earth. At least three arguments echoed through the valley, two of them in languages she barely understood.

A beautiful, dangerous, impossible mess.

Valdek stood beside her, wrapped in his thick oiled cloak, frost clinging stubbornly to the fur at his shoulders. His now-bald head covered with a cap, tidy beard now mostly white, but despite his age his presence hadn't dimmed.

"She's growing too big to hide much longer," he murmured. "Even this far north."

Anya didn't look away from the camp. "We'll have to move again soon."

"Where?" he asked. "The magisters scour the west. The lowland roads are choked with their wagons. If we go further north, the sand tribes will turn on us the moment our backs are turned."

She smirked faintly. "They have already turned on us. Twice."

Valdek grunted. "And yet here they remained."

It was true. The rebellion was a strange beast, stitched together with desperation, revenge, and cold pragmatism.

The Eastern Lancers rode beside the western bandits, sleek and proud, sharing fires with grizzled outlaws who couldn't read their letters, even if it was burned into their skin.

From further north, several dozen members of the Shatter Tooth tribe had pledged their blades. A fierce and reclusive people who were rumoured to eat their dead for strength. Whether that was still true, Anya didn't ask. All that mattered was that they hated the magi more than they hated each other.

And that was enough, at least for now.

Her hand rested on the hilt of her rapier, the same sword Branislav had given her when she had turned twelve. Despite his office and the duty that came with it, he had only ever called her malyshka, *little one*, never Tsarevna.

She missed him most on days like this.

Behind her, the scouts returned through the pass. Their horses lathered and panted.

One of them, a dark, wiry woman from the southern mountains, slid from the saddle and approached with a grim set to her jaw.

"They're moving," she said, voice clipped. "A caravan. Big and heavily guarded."

Anya's eyes narrowed. "Direction?"

"West. Toward the coast. Looks like one of the Blackhold convoys."

Valdek shifted beside her. "Any prisoners?"

The scout nodded. "At least three carts. We couldn't get any closer without being seen."

Anya exhaled slowly, mind already turning. "That means another intake. Another round of experiments."

Valdek's jaw clenched. "And another reason to strike before they reach the bridge."

For a long moment, Anya said nothing. The wind blew cold from the peaks. She would save them this time.

***

Anya had found Captain Haldic at the edge of the training grounds. He was inspecting the lances of his men, but the tight line of his jaw betrayed weariness beyond the physical.

"You move as if you've ridden through a storm you can't outrun," she whispered, stepping into the quiet corner.

He glanced up, surprised to see her there. For a moment, the armour of command fell from him in small ways, his shoulders slumped, his eyes held a shadow of loss. "I suppose I have," he admitted. "The men expect me to be strong, but the mountains are not forgiving to horses or their riders."

Anya nodded, her fingers brushing the edge of a training dummy as she considered her own burdens. "I understand. Every choice, every order, it leaves a mark. I wonder sometimes if it will ever leave me at all."

She looked at him then, and she saw not the captain, not the soldier, but a man who had known deep loss. "We carry it because we must," he said softly. "Even when we'd rather not."

Their eyes met, and for a heartbeat, no words were necessary. The wind stirred, rattling banners and scattering dust across the ground, but between them, there was a fragile understanding.

***

That evening, inside the camp's largest tent, a rough-hewn table was strewn with maps, sketches, and chipped arrows.

Anya stood at the head, her sword rested on the seat behind her, but never far from reach. Around her were the captains, a volatile council forged by necessity more than trust.

Valdek's sharp eyes scanned the faces. Each bore scars, not just of battle, but of old grudges.

To her left, Haldic, the leader of the Eastern Lancers, adjusted the embroidered sash around his chest. His silk-clad demeanour clashed with the dirt under his fingernails. "We cannot delay. The magi convoy will be beyond the pass by the week's end. Our window closes fast."

Near the fire, Banu, a grizzled bandit from the western holds, spat into the brazier. "And what then? You rush past with your lancers, and we're left to burn under magi fire. I won't die for your glory."

From the shadows, Ula leaned forward, pale eyes gleaming like a predator. "Your fear is weakness, Banu. The magi bleed like anyone else."

Valdek's voice cut through. "Enough." A hush fell.

Anya raised a hand. "We may be fractured, but our enemy is bound by cruelty. If we don't strike, others will suffer in our place."

Haldic's gaze swept the circle, lingering on Ula, then Banu. "Then we strike with discipline. My lancers will charge. Bandits in the dark. Hunters on the flanks." His words carried the edge of a man unused to compromise.

Banu growled. "And what of your archers, Tsarevna? Will they watch while we bleed?"

Anya's eyes flashed. "They'll follow my orders. As will you."

Ula's teeth glinted in the firelight. "We fight for those still chained in the Blackhold. For those who cannot choose."

Valdek nodded. "The magisters think High Tower's shadow makes us bow. Let's show them fear cuts both ways."

Banu muttered, "I don't trust cannibals."

Ula's smile curled, sharp and deliberate. "Nor should you."

Anya's voice hardened. "Trust me or leave. The convoy halts at Outpost Vaskor. A fortress, yes, but not untouchable. We'll divide them, bleed them, and free the prisoners before their masters can answer."

Banu leaned forward. "And when they send regiments after us?"

"We'll be gone," Anya shot back. "They'll find only ashes. But if we do nothing, the convoy reaches the Blackhold, and you know what awaits there."

Silence held the circle. Even Banu said no more.

At last, Haldic inclined his head, pride stiff in the motion. "Then we ride. When do we leave?"

Anya looked through the slit of the tent, where the moon rose pale over snow-capped ridges.
"In three nights. Prepare your men. This time, we don't just raid... We send a message."

***

The brazier painted the canvas walls of Anya's command-tent in restless amber. The war-table sat abandoned; outside, captains barked orders and packhorses clattered. Inside, it was quiet except for the soft rustle of feathers.

She stood still in the centre of the tent, left arm extended and braced. Perched upon it was Sokol, her great war-falcon, easily half her size, lighter than he looked, and sharper than anything the blacksmiths in the rebellion could forge. His dark wings twitched with restrained power; talons curled around her thick bracer.

She fed him slivers of salted hare, holding the meat high so he wouldn't lunge. He took them with a click of his beak, swift, but measured. They had learned to trust one another long ago, but trust didn't prevent accidental bites.

Valdek ducked back in through the tent flap. "He looks hungry."

"He always is," Anya replied. "He'd rather be out hunting. We all would."

Valdek eyed the massive bird. "If that thing ever turned on you, I don't think even I could pull it off you in time."

Anya smirked. "Then let's both hope I never give him a reason to."

Sokol shifted, feathers bristling, head tilting as if he understood. Anya stroked the back of his neck carefully, mindful of his mood.

Valdek stepped closer, lowering his voice. "The captains are bristling. Haldic doesn't like riding alongside the Shatter Tooth. Banu's claiming first spoils already. Ula hasn't spoken another word."

"They'll hold," Anya said. "If they want this war to mean anything."

"They want blood. You're the only one who wants order, Tsarevna."

She didn't answer for a moment. Sokol let out a low screech, which sounded too much like an echo of her own frustration. She turned her head, eyes narrowing. "This outpost will be our first test. If we take it together, we continue to move as one. If they fracture... we lose everything."

Valdek's gaze shifted between her and the bird. "And if they try to turn on you?"

"Then I cut their wings before they take flight." She turned and gestured to the perch near the cot. Sokol hopped down with a powerful thud, wings unfurling once before settling, his fierce gaze fixed toward the tent's opening.

"He senses something," Valdek murmured.

"He always does." She pulled off the bracer and flexed her sore fingers. "Sokol's never wrong about danger, unlike my father. I just wish he could tell me what he senses."

"You already know. You just don't want to admit it."

Anya glanced at the map, then at Valdek. "Fetch Ula, quietly. I want to make sure she understands how much of the plan relies on her tribe."

"And the others?"

"One at a time..."

Valdek gave a nod but hesitated. "You've become more like your father than you realise."

She gave him a tired smile. "My father taught me how to wear a crown, my mother how to wear a dress, and Branislav taught me how to hold a blade. But it was you who taught me how to survive."

Valdek chuckled, then turned toward the flap.

Behind her, Sokol let out a low, rising call, almost like a horn. Anya froze for just a moment, then crossed the tent and placed a hand against the falcon's breast, steadying him.

"I know," she whispered. "Soon."

Outside, the rebellion stirred, drawn toward battle. Inside the tent, a warbird waited, feathers rustling like blades in the dark.

                              ***

The tent flap pulled open.

Ula stepped in, silent as snow. Her eyes gleamed pale beneath a hood of stitched bone and hide, and her smile, filled with dagger-filed teeth, was both warming and intense.

"You asked for me."

Anya didn't turn, standing over the large map in the centre of the tent. "You're the only one I trust to do this."

Ula moved closer, gaze sliding over the positions marked in charcoal and crimson. "The sentry towers?"

Anya nodded. "They're worse than watchmen. A single horn blast will echo across these passes," she tapped a thin line of mountains, "and alert outposts days away. If that happens, we lose everything."

Ula grunted. "How many?"

"Four along the ridge. Each within sight of the next. If even one warns the outpost…"

Ula's fingers traced a narrow trail toward the first tower. "Then we silence them. All of them. Quick and quiet."

At last, Anya looked up. "You'll have two hours before the assault. If we see a signal fire or hear a horn…" She gestured to the falcon, which shrieked on cue. "I'll call the attack off."

Ula bared her teeth. "My children will be like wind through the trees. They will not fail."

"I hope not," Anya said coolly. "Because if they do, the magi will destroy everything we've built."

For a moment, only the crackle of the fire filled the tent. Then Anya spoke again, quieter. "Ula… many call your people fanatics. Some whisper cannibals. Does that not anger you?"

Ula turned, her gaze cold as a glacier. Anya braced, but then Ula laughed, sharp and sudden.

"Fanatics, cannibals, monsters. They may call us what they will. We do not break so easily. We Shatter Tooth worship the Pale Queen, Lady of Death. To others, death is something to fear. To us, it is sacred. To fight, to bleed, to die, all are gifts that she gives. Fear itself is her gift."

Her pale eyes caught the firelight, glinting with something fierce and unreadable. "Why should I be insulted by what they fear?"

Anya held her gaze, uncertain if she was reassured or unsettled. Whatever else Ula was, she was unshakable.

Without another word, Ula turned and vanished into the night, a shadow among shadows.

***

The flap of the tent had barely settled behind Ula's retreating form when another silhouette stepped into view. Tall, broad-shouldered, with a cavalryman's posture that betrayed years in the saddle.

Captain Haldic.

He gave a respectful nod to the guards flanking the entrance before stepping in. Behind him, Sokol tilted his head and let out a low hiss.

Anya stood still, her hand braced against the edge of the table. She didn't turn at first, only lifted her cup and drank deeply.

"Captain."

"Tsarevna," he greeted, voice calm and composed.

Anya sighed and set the cup back down, her shoulders heavy. "Do you ever get tired, Haldic? Not in the way battle wears you down, but in your bones. In your soul."

He did not answer at once. He stepped closer, eyes on the map. "Tired or not, the raid must go forward."

"I know." She rubbed her temple with the heel of her hand. "The Stags know their part. Ula's taken hers. And your lancers will sweep in once the towers fall."

He gave a single, steady nod. "We'll be ready."

Anya's gaze lingered on the map, though her thoughts had already left it behind. At length, she looked at the two guards stationed within. "Leave us."

They exchanged a glance but obeyed without question, stepping outside as the flap fell shut.

The tent was silent. Anya crossed to the wine, poured a fresh cup, and let it rest untouched in her hand. Her eyes met Haldic's across the firelight. No words passed between them.

Her hand drifted to the cords of her shirt, loosening them with measured calm. Sokol shifted his wings. The war map behind them stood untouched, tokens still locked in place, waiting for dawn.

***

The first light of dawn crept into the tent like a cautious thief, silvering the edges of the furs and casting long, pale shadows across the floor. The brazier's glow had faded to smouldering embers, and the falcon perched silently, watching from its stand with a predator's patience.

Next to Anya, the bed was empty. Haldic having slipped out during the night, leaving only the faintest impression on the furs.

A soft rustle at the entrance broke the stillness.

"Tsarevna," came Valdek's voice, low and respectful.

Anya stirred, blinking as her body reminded her of its weariness. She sat up slowly, brushing a curl of dark hair from her face. "What time is it?"

"Just past first light. The Stags are already preparing, and Ula's scouts returned not long ago. It's time."

She gave a tired nod and rose, wrapping a thick woollen shawl around her shoulders before stepping behind the tall privacy screen near her cot.

Valdek remained by the tent's entrance, facing out of the tent, out of courtesy, arms folded. The tension in his posture had not eased. The day ahead would be hard, and he knew it.

"Did you sleep?" she asked from behind the screen. The sound of leather cords being tightened followed her voice.

"Not enough." A pause. "Did Haldic leave?"

She stepped out, dressed in a simple wool tunic beneath a sleeveless coat reinforced with boiled leather. Strapping on her sword belt, which held the basket hilt of her sword. Tucking her ornate dagger into its sheath. "Sometime after midnight. I didn't ask him to stay."

Valdek studied her face, searching for something perhaps, but said nothing. She offered a faint smile that didn't quite reach her eyes.

"Let's see if our rebels are awake," she said, stepping out into the crisp morning air.

Outside, the camp was already coming to life. Smoke rose from cooking fires, the clatter of hooves and armour mixing with indistinct murmurs. The Eastern Lancers were strapping their ornate banners to their saddles, with two per horseman, angled to soar behind them like wings. The Shatter Tooth sharpened their short blades. The Stags tightened saddle straps and checked their bows and curved blades.

Anya stepped up onto the small rise overlooking the camp. The gathered rebels quieted as she raised her voice, the wind tugging at her cloak.

"You've all come here from different lands, under different banners. Some of you rode with my father. Some of you ran with wolves. And some of you," her gaze flicked to the Shatter Tooth warriors and the tattered remnants of Banu's bandits, "have never sworn loyalty to anything but your gods."

She paused, letting that truth settle. Then her voice sharpened.

"But today, we stand together. Not for gold. Not for conquest. But because the magisters think they can take and burn and shackle, and that there is no one left to rise and stop them."

A murmur of assent rippled through the ranks.

"They are wrong!"

Sokol gave a cry, high and piercing, as if echoing her words.

"We ride for every prisoner in their chains. We ride for every village turned to ash. For every name they tried to erase. For every child raised to fear their own voice."

She drew her rapier in a slow, deliberate motion.

"Make them remember us. Make them regret ever thinking we were broken."

She raised the blade, and her voice. "We ride!"

Chapter Five

The air in the Blackhold never changed. Damp, heavy with salt and soot, laced with decay. Time blurred in the dark, unlit chambers. Days meant nothing. There was only before and after.

Before the pain and after the experiments.

Daran didn't remember how long it had been since he'd last seen Tareq or his father. Maybe weeks, maybe months. His cell was little more than a metal box, barely wide enough to lie down in, sealed with a solid earthen steel door. Meals came at irregular intervals. There was no light, no warmth, only the cold press of steel and silence.

Footsteps. Heavy boots. The scrape of a bolt.

"On your feet," came the voice of a handler.

The sudden brightness stabbed his eyes. He was thinner and hollow-eyed now, but he obeyed. He didn't want to be dragged again. Chains clinked as he stood.

They took him through winding corridors, past pipes that hissed with steam and doors that hummed with unnatural energy, until they reached the chamber.

Fleshwright Ildran was already there, waiting.

His pale robe swept the floor like a veil of death. His face untouched by time, his eyes sterile and curious. The faint clinking beneath his robe echoed with each shift.

Daran's mouth was dry. His wrist throbbed, not in pain, but pressure, where his missing hand had once been.

The replacement was a mockery of flesh. Alchemically infused earth shaped into crude bone and sinew, set into his wrist like splinters of stone. The skin of his wrist was discoloured, ridged with scar tissue. The fingers twitched involuntarily.

"Sit," the magister said.

He obeyed.

A table was placed before him, etched with runes and scattered with tiny rods and weights. Dexterity drills.

"Begin."

Daran reached. His flesh fingers trembled with fatigue, the stone ones stiff, out of sync. He tried to grasp a rod. It slipped, clattering loudly. A cold ache travelled up his arm.

The magister watched. "It must become natural. You are one of only three survivors from this trial. The essence takes hold slowly, but it will take hold."

Daran's jaw clenched. "I'm not some puppet or golem that can blindly be commanded."

"No," the magister murmured, his expression unchanged. "Not yet."

He drifted aside. "Continue."

Daran bent again to the task, his hand jerked clumsily over the puzzle.

The chamber was quiet save for the clink of stone on brass and the whisper of the Blackhold itself. It was alive, and hungry.

The magister's gaze narrowed as another rod slipped from Daran's grip. With a silent gesture, the chamber door opened.

"Bring in the other."

The guard returned with a man who moved like a shadow crawling across scorched earth. The left side of his face was a melted ruin, his right arm wrapped in scorched leather.

Despite it all, he grinned.

"Well, look at you," he rasped. "Only a hand? You got off easy."

Daran froze at the voice.

"Tareq…"

"In the charred flesh."

"What did they…"

"Fire essence." He tapped his chest with a blackened thumb. "Tried to turn me into a walking furnace. Mostly worked." His laugh was dry as ash. "You should see the ones who didn't make it."

The magister circled them, silent except for the metallic clink. "Proximity may produce resonance. Harmony or dissonance, it matters not." He motioned to the table. "Continue."

Tareq dropped onto a bench, his grin crooked. "So, earth essence, huh? What's it like?"

"Wrong," Daran muttered. "Heavy. Dead."

"Could be worse." Tareq lifted his ruined arm, then let it fall. "You could feel everything."

Before Daran could answer, the chamber door burst open. A guard stumbled in, a lantern swinging in his hand.

"Fleshwright! Outpost Vaskor's been hit. The convoy was intercepted. The prisoners are gone. They're moving west. Toward us!"

The magister turned his head slowly, the metallic clinking growing sharper.

Tareq's grin widened. "Well now. Isn't that interesting?"

He got to his feet and staggered off-balance, colliding with the startled guard. The lantern slipped from his grasp. As it fell, Tareq kicked it against the wall, glass fracturing, oil spilling.

Flames leapt upwards.

"Oops," Tareq rasped, but there was no humour now, only venom. He raised both arms. Leather split. His ruined skin glowed like coals, his fingers flexed as fire bent toward him, coiling into a molten orb.

"This is for my dad," he hissed. "And the Stags who fell."

The orb split, slamming into guard and magister alike. Fire roared. The magister's robe caught, flaring like parchment, the clink beneath hissing to life.

As the flames climbed, six metallic spider-like limbs punched free, essence capsules glowing blue and white at the joints.

"Go!" Tareq barked. "Now!"

Daran obeyed.

They tore through the corridors, smoke clinging to their clothes.

"We need to get out before they lock this place down," Tareq hissed.

"I'm not leaving without my father. He's in the forges."

Tareq cursed, but nodded. "Fine. Then move."

Two guards rounded a corner, swords drawn, but behind them, faint glowing lines shimmered along the stone floor. The runes etched into the walls flared, a pulse of cold energy crackling toward them. Tareq flung his flames just as the first ward snapped, searing sparks against the stone. One guard screamed, his flesh seared to his armour. The other ran, smoke and light consuming him.

A massive flagstone smashed down from above, crushing him. Blood sprayed, acrid in the smoke.

Tareq spun. Daran stood behind him, chest heaving, stone hand still gripping rubble like it weighed nothing.

"I was holding back for the magi," Daran said, his voice flat.

Tareq grinned savagely. "Well don't hold back now."

***

The forge halls were a world of their own. Vaulted ceilings invisible in the smoke. Rows of furnaces glowed. Chains rattled. No cries, no voices. Only the hammer's dirge.

Discarded tools lay scattered in heaps, iron worn smooth by a thousand hands.

Tareq slowed at the entrance. "A graveyard filled with fire."

Daran pushed forward. "We'll split up, we can cover more ground."

Tareq peeled left, weaving through sparks and smoke. Daran stalked the aisles, searching every face.

To his right, steel flashed. A guard lunged toward him. Daran raised his stone hand, and the blade rang against it, sparks spitting. Using his free hand, he seized a chunk of slag and drove it into the man's face. The guard collapsed, his helmet crumpled, his screams faded in the roar of the furnaces.

Eyes turned toward him.

"Where is Boran?" His voice cut through the haze. "The master smith?"

A trembling hand pointed toward a side chamber that glow red.

***

Inside, the Fleshwright waited.

His robe was scorched, his face blistered, his metal limbs blackened but steady. In his hand, a rod of glowing steel pressed close to Boran's throat.

The old man hung by his chains. He was battered but still upright. One of his eyes was swollen shut, but still burned with hatred.

"I knew you'd come," the magister rasped. "You look just like him."

Daran took a step forward.

The magister pressed the bar closer. Boran winced from the heat but lifted his head. His one good eye found Daran's. Steady and unflinching. A faint nod.

"Father…"

"You've undone more than you know," the magister hissed.

Boran gave a small smile despite the situation. "That's my boy…" he began, but with sudden fury, Ildran plunged the iron into his throat.

Chains rattled as his body sagged.

Daran staggered. His world blurred around him. His scream tore loose but was swallowed by the roar of fire and grief.

His hand tightened on the blood-slicked slag. He hurled it.

The magister batted it aside with a metal limb, the stone cracking into the wall.

"You are promising," he said. "But still so very small."

A capsule pulsed brightly on his leg, and lightning fired out, blasting the chamber apart. Daran dove, barely ahead of it, crashing behind an anvil. His father's new anvil. Memories surged back to him. Their mark etched deeply long ago.

And there, half-buried in debris and soot, lay a hammer. Broad-headed, haft worn smooth. His father's hammer.

He seized it.

His stone fingers bit into the floor and tore loose a flagstone. He rose, a roar building in his chest, and tossed the stone upwards.

Stone met steel in one explosive motion. The hammer strike sang like thunder, launching the rock like a meteor. It smashed into the magister's shoulder, tearing a limb free in a burst of sparks.

The whole chamber shook, its walls cracked.

Daran lowered the hammer, his face set like stone.

The forge itself groaned. Rubble fell. Prisoners scattered, some seizing tools, others striking at guards in a desperate frenzy. The rebellion was fire now, spreading through the prisoners, uncontrolled.

The magister reeled, shrieking, his shoulder sparking.

Daran's eyes locked on Boran's body. His grip tightened on the hammer.

"Daran!"

Tareq burst in, flames writhing around him. He saw the body, the magister, the spreading cracks. "We have to go!"

"He killed him," Daran growled.

Tareq seized his arm. "And if you stay, he'll kill you too!" Daran wrenched back, nearly breaking free, fury radiating off him.

Another crack thundered overhead. The ceiling began to collapse.

"Move!" Tareq roared, dragging him through the storm of debris. Behind them, the magister's shriek rose, then was swallowed by the collapse.

***

Across the forge, prisoners fought and fell, hammers clanged against armoured guards. Others fled into the smoke, dragging chains still clamped to their ankles. Fire licked across scaffolds. The drive to fight burned within them.

"This way!" a soot-covered prisoner shouted from the archway. "There's a tunnel past the scrap bay. It exits near the gate!"

They sprinted, ducking falling beams, weaving between ward traps and guards. The hammer still clutched tightly in Daran's grip, his legs burned from moving with such pace, unknown to him for what felt like a lifetime. Sparks and fire skittered across stone in the deadly storm behind them.

The forge roared, a furnace of death and defiance, as they vanished into the dark, alive only by the narrowest margin.

Chapter Six

The wind off the sea howled between the sheer cliffs, carrying the tang of smoke and iron.

Anya reined in her horse at the crest of the road, her eyes fixed on the bridge that led to the Blackhold. The ancient span arched over the churning waters below, its black stone slick from the spray.

Behind her, the column of rebels, a patchwork of farmers, hardened fighters, deserters and freed prisoners from Outpost Vaskor. They marched in loose formation, accompanied by her existing forces. The clatter of mismatched weapons and scavenged armour echoed across the barren plains.

Ula approached Anya silently, her face full of concern.

"Tsarevna, my people won't go any closer to that place, it is forbidden by the Pale Queen."

Anya met her gaze. "I will not ask the Shatter Tooth to go against their goddess."

Ula's voice dropped. "You don't understand. We call it the Tomb of the Deathless Ones. It is a desecration of her gift."

Before Anya could reply, the Blackhold stirred.

With a groan of iron and stone, the gates slammed wide, but no guards stood beyond. Her stomach knotted. Open gates rarely meant good news. "Ready weapons!" she called. Shields lifted, bows sat knocked.

Then figures poured through them, but not to attack. Magister guards fled in broken ranks. Their faces twisted in terror. Behind them came a flood of ragged prisoners, shackles still dragging behind them. At their head ran a man wreathed in fire, and beside him a broad-shouldered figure clutching a hammer in one hand, his other a fist of stone.

The column of rebels stiffened, voices falling silent. Men and women shifted nervously, tightened their grip on spear hafts, settled helmets into place and passed quick glances at one another.

Anya narrowed her eyes at the open passageway ahead. Either the Blackhold had fallen, or something inside wanted them to enter.

"Hold your ground!" she barked and circled in front of her forces. Her makeshift army stood silently, hearts pounding toward whatever waited beyond the gates.

Dust and rubble poured from its towers as the great prison started to collapse in on itself.

Anya's eyes widened as she realised who the men at the front must be and what they had done.

Kicking her heels into her horse, she spurred it forward, steel flashed as she drew her rapier.

"Hold the bridge!" she shouted over her shoulder to her forces. "Clear the way!"

Her horse thundered toward the fleeing mass, the open gates of the collapsing Blackhold looming behind them.

***

Anya met the first of the magister guards in full stride, her horse surged beneath her as she leaned low in the saddle. Her rapier punched down through the soft gap between helm and gorget, the steel easily sliding through flesh before bursting from the man's back. He crumpled with a gurgle, his sword clattering to the stone.

She wrenched her blade free, the point snapping up into a defensive guard just in time to catch the edge of a wild, panicked swing from another soldier. The clash of steel rang sharply in her ears. She twisted her wrist, rolling the attack aside, then stepped in and drove her rapier forward in a single, clean thrust. The point found the narrow slit in the man's visor. His whole body went stiff, a startled gasp echoed inside the helm, and then he sagged lifelessly and toppled backward as she pulled free.

She pivoted to search for the next threat and caught movement in the corner of her eye. Another soldier was charging in from her flank, their sword raised high for a killing blow. She could not bring her blade from her current opponent to meet it in time.

A piercing cry split the air.

From the dark, cloud-filled sky above, Sokol swooped like a thunderbolt, his wings folded tight. His talons locked around the guard's head and shoulders, the sheer force of the impact lifting the man off his feet. His scream was lost beneath the rush of air as the falcon's wings flared wide, carrying him toward the edge of the bridge. A heartbeat later, Sokol released him, and the guard tumbled helplessly into the churning, rock-strewn sea far below.

The guard's retreat faltered. Some stumbled to a halt, torn between the terror behind them and the deadly figure in front. Anya did not give them the chance to decide.

Her sword became a silver thread in the air, weaving between parries and thrusts, finding the gaps in armour, exploiting their fear. Each kill was swift and without hesitation, her expression cold and unreadable. Blood slicked the stones underfoot as the chaos of the bridge grew, the thunder of boots, the ring of steel, and the desperate cries of those caught between collapsing fortress and merciless foe.

The wind off the ocean tore at her hair and cloak, but Anya pressed forward, a single point of deadly precision in the roiling chaos, she cut down every man in her path.

***

Anya wrenched her blade free from the last of the magister guard, his body collapsing in a heap at her feet. The bridge was littered with the fallen, their weapons abandoned where they had slipped from lifeless hands. She turned, breathing hard, her eyes sweeping over the ragged column of freed prisoners spilling from the gates of the Blackhold.

"Follow me to safety," she shouted, her voice cutting through the chaos like a whip crack.

The call carried across the bridge, rising above the roar of the collapsing fortress and the distant shouts of battle. For a heartbeat they wavered, glancing back at the ruin. Then, step by step, they surged toward her. Anya kicked her horse into motion, riding back toward her forces, her rapier raised and eyes fierce. "Keep moving, don't look back!" she barked. The authority in her voice left no room for doubt or delay.

The first to respond were the strongest among them. Men and women broken by toil in the magister's service, who pulled the slower and weaker along. The column flowed toward her, gathering speed as the ground behind them shuddered with another deep, echoing rumble. Dust and stone plumed into the air as another section of the Blackhold gave way, its towers tilting and breaking apart before vanishing into a haze of rubble.

Anya kept her horse moving along the line, making herself a clear beacon to follow. Sokol weaved under and above the bridge, his sharp cries herding stragglers toward the centre. Every step away from the fortress was a step toward survival, and she would not allow any hesitation to cost them their lives.

The prisoners surged after her, leaving the ruin of their prison behind.

***

Anya swung down from her saddle the moment they cleared the far side of the bridge, her boots hitting the dirt with a thud. She immediately began issuing orders, her voice cutting across the chaos of the scene.

"See to the wounded," she shouted, pointing toward a line of carts. "Put those who cannot walk onto horses or wagons. Give food and water to the rest. Keep them moving and keep them breathing."

Her fighters moved quickly, peeling away to tend to the prisoners. Some were lifting the injured onto carts, others were tearing strips of cloth from their own cloaks to use as bandages. The air was heavy with the sounds of exhaustion, coughing and groaning mixing with the quiet words of comfort from those tending the pain.

Then the crowd stilled.

It started at the edge closest to the bridge and spread through the ranks until the entire group looked to the span of stone. Anya felt the change and turned as well, her hand resting on the hilt of her rapier.

Three figures were making their way across. The first was Fleshwright Ildran, his pale robes burnt and torn, parts of his body blackened from fire. The metal limbs struck the bridge with sharp, deliberate impacts, each step echoed in the stillness.

Beside him walked another figure in pale robes, a woman who moved with a calm and deliberate grace. Her hood was back, and her eyes were fixed forward, glimmering like cold glass. Her hands were clasped in front of her as though she held something dangerous.

Between them came an elderly man in crimson robes. His back was slightly bent, yet his pace never faltered. A long white beard moved in the wind as the staff in his hand tapped against the bridge with each step. His presence carried a quiet power that made the nearest rebels shift their footing as if bracing for a blow.

The three advanced without hurry, despite the Blackhold collapsing in ruins behind them. Dust and ash swirled in the wind, and Anya's grip on her sword tightened.

This was far from finished.

***

Fleshwright Ildran halted halfway across the bridge, his scorched robes whipped in the wind. His heavy mechanical legs clanked against the stone as he planted himself firmly, his front two legs raised, and pointed at the gathered crowd. His voice erupted in fury, carrying across the ruined span.

"You have broken the last bulwark." He shouted, his eyes blazed with rage. "What comes next is on your head, not ours."

His words echoed off the cliffs and the water below, hanging heavy in the air like an ill omen. The rebels fell silent, the weight of his anger pressing down on them as the ruins of the fortress behind him finally lay still.

Anya met his gaze with unwavering resolve. She drew and levelled her rapier steadily at the three approaching magisters, her voice ringing out with unshakable authority.

"These people are under my protection," she declared, her words sharp and clear. "By the name of Tsarevna Anya Velmira, none of you may pass."

The words rang across the battered bridge, cutting through the tension like a blade. The rebels behind her stiffened, their eyes flicking nervously between the ruined fortress and the looming figures.

Suddenly, she sensed movement beside her, a shift in the air. Her eyes snapped sideways to see two figures stepping forward to join her.

The first was the burned man, his skin marked by scars and seared flesh, yet his eyes burned bright with fierce determination. Flames danced softly around him, casting an eerie glow that clung to his form like a living cloak.

At his side was the dark-skinned man. Calm and steady, his stone prosthetic hand gleamed even in the dim light. His gaze was measured but resolute, carrying the weight of everything he had endured.

The burned man's lips curled into a wide grin, a rare expression of triumph in a world that was now so full of hardship and pain. He fixed Anya with a fierce look from his remaining eye and spoke, voice low, rasping voice.

"These ones are ours."

Anya's grip tightened on the rapier's hilt, the leather wrap cool against her palm. Her gaze flicked from the magisters to the two men who had fought their way through fire and torment to stand beside her now.

Around them, the murmurs of the rebels grew louder, hope rekindling, courage swelling.

The air thickened with the promise of battle but also with the fragile hope that, together, they might finally turn the tide.

The magister's voice cut across the growing tension with two simple words.

"Then die."

***

Ildran's metal legs pointed directly at the rebels glowed with a fierce light. Daran's breath caught in his throat as the familiar surge of dread filled him. He knew what was coming.

Daran's body moved before thought. His feet hammering stone, he planted himself between the magisters and the rebels.

"Daran, what are you doing?" a shout cut through the tension, urgent and filled with alarm.

Guilt burned in his chest. He would not fail again. His palm slammed the ground. The bridge heaved, stone and dust twisted into a wall. Lightning struck stone with a crash like thunder, but the shield held. Sparks spat into the air.

Behind the wall, the rebels exhaled, some stepping forward with renewed hope. Daran stayed low for a moment longer, sweat beaded on his brow, he felt the pulse of the earth beneath his hand.

As the sharp scent of ozone slowly faded from the air, Tareq launched into motion. He sprinted toward the towering earthen shield that Daran had just raised. Flames flickered wildly in both of his hands, growing brighter and hotter with every step, their warm glow contrasting with the pale twilight.

"Lower the wall!" Tareq's voice rang out, cutting through the tension like a blade.

Daran's eyes locked onto Tareq's approach. Though surprised by the sudden command, he nodded without hesitation. The wall before him, a solid bulwark moments ago, began to shift as he loosened his control over the earth.

As Tareq neared the shield, a portion of it suddenly crumbled, stone and soil tumbling down in a controlled collapse. The gap created a perfect step, a launching pad carved from the very earth itself.

Without breaking stride, Tareq leapt onto the broken section of the wall, his body rising in a powerful arc. The flames wrapped around him like living ribbons, twisting and swirling with a fierce intensity.

At the peak of his jump, time seemed to slow. Tareq stretched out both hands, gathering the fire into tight spheres of blazing energy. With a sharp exhale, he hurled the fireballs forward, sending them streaking through the air toward the magisters.

The fiery orbs raced ahead, trailing sparks and flickers of smoke, cutting through the cold air like shooting stars.

The elderly magister lifted his staff with deliberate force and called out, "Aereos!"

The air surrounding him rippled and twisted, responding to his command. In an instant, a swirling wall of invisible wind sprang to life, coiling tightly around him and the metal-legged magister like a living barrier. The shield hummed with power, bending the currents of the air and crackling faintly as it absorbed the heat and flames from the incoming fireballs.

Protected within this swirling tempest, the two magisters stood firm, their expressions unreadable behind scorched robes and grim determination.

But the third magister was not so lucky. One fireball found its mark, exploding against her with a sudden roar. Flames leapt up her sleeves and across her body, engulfing her in a violent blaze. Her eyes widened in shock and pain as the fire consumed her robes and skin alike.

The blast threw her backward with brutal force, into the stone barrier of the bridge. She tumbled over the edge, her form swallowed by smoke and flame as she fell into the swirling foam far below.

The sudden disappearance of a magister sent a ripple of shock through both sides. The air hung heavy with the smell of smoke and the crackle of dying embers, but the battle was far from over.

***

Valdek moved closer to Anya, lowering his voice to a quiet urgency. The recently freed prisoners were scattered across the bridge and nearby paths, many exhausted or injured. Their makeshift army was weary, and their numbers were stretched thin.

"Tsarevna, we should consider a strategic retreat," Valdek said, his eyes scanning the ragged faces of their fighters. "Our first responsibility must be the safety of these people. We cannot risk everything on a battle we might not win. If we pull back now, we preserve our strength and live to fight another day."

Anya turned slowly, her gaze steady and unflinching. The weight of leadership pressed down on her shoulders, but in her eyes burned a fierce determination that had only grown sharper over the years.

"We have come too far to turn back now," she said, her voice calm but resolute. "If we retreat now, everything we have sacrificed, every life lost, will be for nothing."

She stepped forward, scanning the faces of those around her; the weary, the hopeful, the broken. "These people depend on us. Their freedom is not just a gift; it is a promise. We owe it to them, to ourselves, to see this through. No matter the cost."

Anya's gaze sharpened as she faced her trusted commanders, the weight of the moment settling heavily upon her. She took a steadying breath before issuing her orders, her voice clear and commanding.

"Valdek," she began, fixing her eyes on him, "you will take charge of the retreat. You must prioritise the safety of the freed people. Guide them swiftly and quietly away from this place, using every hidden path we have scouted. No one, no matter how injured or weak, is to be left behind. I trust your judgment to keep them safe."

Valdek nodded solemnly, the weight of responsibility settling easily on his shoulders.

Turning to Haldic, Anya's tone grew sharper. "You and your lancers will hold the rear guard. Make your stand at the bridge and delay any pursuers for as long as possible. Use the narrow terrain and the ruins to your advantage. Every second you buy will save lives."

Haldic's expression hardened with determination, already calculating the best points to fortify and defend.

Finally, Anya turned to Ula. "Ula, your people know the northern passes better than anyone. Lead the Shatter Tooth in guiding the wounded and those who cannot keep up through the hidden trails. Keep them safe and bring them to our camp. Your knowledge of the land will be their salvation."

Ula's pale eyes met Anya's with a silent promise of fierce protection.

Anya's voice softened slightly but carried the weight of resolve. "I will stay behind as long as I can. I will buy you time."

The commanders exchanged determined glances, the gravity of the plan clear to all. Each knew that their roles were vital, not just for this moment but for the future of the rebellion itself.

***

As the swirling wind barrier surrounding the magisters dissipated, the air grew still and heavy with anticipation. Daran lowered himself briefly, palms pressing into the cracked stone beneath him. Slowly, the earth responded, shifting and rising to form a thick, protective layer encasing his entire arm. The rough surface hardened quickly, forming a sturdy shield that gleamed with the muted brown glow of earthen essence.

He glanced back at Tareq, his voice low but resolute. "Stay behind me." His resolve in his tone left no room for argument.

Tareq's eyes narrowed with concern, but he nodded and stepped forward to fall in line directly behind Daran. The weight of what was to come pressed on both, yet neither faltered.

Anya moved up beside them, her rapier still held in her hand. The faintest gleam caught the fading light as she drew near. She met Tareq's gaze, noticing the worry etched across his face. "You should stay behind," he hissed, his voice edged with urgency.

Anya shook her head slowly, a small but fierce smile playing at her lips. "What kind of leader would I be if I ran while others fought on my behalf?" She said softly but with unwavering conviction.

For a moment, the three of them stood there united yet aware of the danger that awaited. Then, with slow and deliberate steps, they advanced across the bridge. The tension in the air was palpable, every sound amplified, the crunch of their feet on stone, the distant crackle of magic, the crash of waves far below.

As Daran charged forward across the bridge, the Fleshwright pivoted with unsettling precision. The glowing segment on one of his mechanical limbs pulsed a deep, royal blue, casting an eerie light over the cracked stones beneath them. The magister lifted the leg slowly, aiming it directly at Daran's advancing form.

Without warning, a torrent of water erupted from the magister's leg, surging forward like a relentless wave unleashed from a stormy sea. The water roared as it barrelled toward Daran, a force meant to sweep him off his feet.

Daran's breath caught for a split second, but his reflexes were faster. He dropped his left arm to his right side, swinging the earthen shield encasing his prosthetic hand in a powerful backhand motion. The solid stone barrier met the rushing water with a thunderous clash, altering its course sharply away from him and those standing just behind.

The redirected torrent slammed against the bridge's edge, sending up sprays of mist that glittered in the pale morning light. Droplets scattered like fractured glass, soaking the worn stone and momentarily masking the grim expressions on the faces watching from both sides.

Despite the deluge, Daran's resolve did not waver. He pressed forward, every step steady and determined, the weight of Ora and his father's deaths driving him onward toward the awaiting magisters.

As they pressed forward, Tareq gathered his power with fierce concentration. Flames danced in his palms before he launched two more fireballs in wide, sweeping arcs around the backs of the magisters. The blazing spheres hissed and crackled, trailing sparks as they raced across the cracked stones of the bridge toward their target.

The elderly magister with the staff reacted instantly. With a swift, practiced motion, he raised his weapon high above his head and bellowed, "Terras!"

The earth within the bridge responded with a deafening roar. A massive pillar of stone erupted suddenly, surging upward from the cracked floor like a living wall. It towered between the magisters and the incoming fire, blocking the flames in a shower of sparks and cracked rock. The pillar's surface was jagged and rough, a stark reminder of the raw elemental power the magister commanded.

The magister's focus was entirely consumed by maintaining the pillar. His eyes flickered with strain as he poured his strength into keeping the stone barrier intact, unaware of the danger creeping closer.

Anya saw her opening and wasted no time. She surged forward with the precision and grace of a seasoned warrior. Her rapier, slender and sharp, moved in a deadly arc. In one fluid motion, she delivered a crosswise slash across the magister's throat.

The magister's eyes widened in shock as the blade bit deep. His body jerked violently, a strangled gasp escaping his lips. Blood welled as he staggered backward, clutching at the wound. The pillar trembled and cracked at its base, pieces of stone breaking loose and falling away.

The sudden falter in the magister's control caused the earth barrier to weaken, the once-imposing wall beginning to crumble. The tide of battle shifted in that moment.

The magister's death shattered the fragile balance between them. The moment his life drained away, his control over the stone vanished. The towering pillar that had risen moments before began to tremble violently, fissures racing across its surface like spiderwebs under pressure. With a roar like grinding boulders, the pillar cracked apart and collapsed, sending shards of rock plummeting into the dark waters far below.

Beneath their feet, the bridge groaned in protest. Cracks spread swiftly, widening gaps swallowing entire sections of stone. Dust and debris filled the air, and the sound of crumbling masonry echoed like thunder through the narrow mountain pass.

Daran's gaze snapped to the advancing figure of the metal-legged magister. His mechanical limbs pumped with relentless force, one leg raised high, poised to bring a crushing blow down upon Anya.

Without hesitation, Daran lunged forward, wrapping his arms tightly around Anya's waist. He yanked her backward just as the magister's leg slammed down where she had stood seconds before, shattering the stone to rubble. The impact sent a shockwave through the bridge, dust clouding the air between them.

"We need to go," Daran hissed urgently, his breath ragged but determined.

There was no time to argue. The three of them turned as one and sprinted away from the collapsing span, their feet pounding the cracked stone as the bridge convulsed beneath them.

Behind them, the ancient structure broke in earnest. Large chunks fell into the sea below with sickening crashes, the narrow path they had just crossed disappearing piece by piece.

Ildran pushed himself forward with furious determination, his mechanical legs churning to keep pace. But as the bridge buckled, one of his legs caught in a crevice. The grinding of metal against stone rang sharply as he struggled to free himself.

The gap widened further, swallowing the leg, then the joint, then the rest of his frame as the bridge gave way beneath him. With a final, ear-splitting screech, the magister was swallowed by the chasm, disappearing from sight.

Panting, the three rebels reached the safety of the cliff's edge, their chests heaving with exertion and relief. They turned to look back at the fractured ruin behind them.

The bridge hung in pieces over the void, swaying precariously in the cold mountain wind.

The Fleshwright was gone.

No more lightning. No more pounding metal. Only the roar of the waves crashing on the rocks below, and their own ragged breathing.

Chapter Seven

Several days had passed since the smoke and screams of the Blackhold faded into the cold wind. The charred remains of the fortress still haunted Anya's mind, the smell of burning pitch clinging stubbornly to her memory. The three of them rode hard along a narrow, rutted trail that wound through the ash-covered fields that were once prosperous farmlands.

Tareq rode ahead, his gaze never still. He constantly scanned the ridgelines with unrelenting vigilance. Daran followed close behind Anya, his jaw tight with the strain of keeping his weary gelding moving. The animal's sides heaved with each breath, and its hooves clopped dully against the frozen ground.

The road north felt endless. Their world had shrunk to the rhythm of hoofbeats, the sting of cold air in their lungs, and the constant prickle of fear at the back of the neck. Twice they had spotted distant patrols, but each time the trio had cut away into thickets or crawled into shallow gullies, hearts hammering, until the danger passed.

The further north they rode, the thinner the air became, and the landscape changed. The open plains gave way to low hills scattered with trees that whispered in the wind like conspirators. Beyond those hills rose the white-capped peaks of the distant mountains, sharp against the grey sky. Somewhere in those mountains, the rebel camp lay hidden, its location known to only their existing forces.

Every mile they put behind them brought no comfort. Anya could feel it like a weight between her shoulder blades. They were being hunted. She clutched her reins tighter, her knuckles pale against the leather.

A crow followed them for a time, its black wings beating lazily overhead, calling harshly in the still air, before being chased off by Sokol. By nightfall, they had reached a shallow creek, the water crusted with ice along its edges. Despite the cold, they dared not light a fire. The three huddled closely in their cloaks, eating hardtack and salted meat while the wind whispered through the dead grass. Sleep came in fits, broken by the sound of shifting hooves or the snap of a branch in the dark.

***

The path opened slowly, the dense forest giving way to a wide, sheltered valley nestled between two towering peaks. Smoke curled lazily from campfires, twisting upward toward a pale sky streaked with clouds. The scent of smoke and damp earth filled the air, mingling with the sharp tang of pine and the distant murmur of voices.

The camp sprawled across the valley floor in a patchwork of tents, lean-tos, and makeshift shelters built from timber and stone. Flags and banners fluttered on hastily erected poles, some marked with the stag's head, others with the crude symbols of the Shatter Tooth and the lancers from the east. Worn but determined faces peered out from doorways, their eyes flicking toward the approaching riders with an equal mixture of hope and caution.

Anya slowed her mount and scanned the camp, her heart tightened. The cost of the recent battle was written on every face, on the stiff limbs of those still recovering, and in the quiet grief held behind clenched jaws. Yet beneath the exhaustion, their determination still burned silently in their eyes. This was no broken band of survivors. This was a gathering storm.

A young scout broke from the shadows and rode forward wearing a leather jerkin patched with a mismatch of old armour. He raised a hand in greeting.

"Tsarevna," he said, voice low but steady, "Your council awaits you."

Daran and Tareq dismounted next to Anya. As they passed between the rows of tents, the murmur of conversation softened, and men and women stepped aside, eyes lingering on the two newcomers with curiosity.

Near the centre of the camp, a circle of rough-hewn logs around a brazier formed a meeting place. Around it stood the leaders of the rebellion.

Anya approached slowly and nodded to each, her gaze remaining on Haldic just a little too long.

"We survived the Blackhold and freed the captives from both there and the nearby outpost," she said, voice clear despite the weariness. "But the war is far from over. The magisters still hold too much power, too many secrets. We must continue fighting to break their hold and free those still under their control."

Her words stirred something in the gathered throng of rebels and prisoners.

Tareq's breath caught as he approached the council. The firelight flickered against the scarred flesh and bandaged arm.

"Banu al-Sayf?" His hoarse voice cut through the frosty night air, trembling slightly with disbelief.

Banu started, turning slowly toward the voice. His gaze locked on Tareq, but the man's face was almost unrecognizable beneath the scars and burnt flesh. For a long moment, the bandit's hand hovered near the curved blade at his side. Then, with a fluid motion, he drew the steel, his blade gleamed with deadly promise.

"Who calls my name?" Banu growled, his voice rough but laced with suspicion and caution.

Tareq took a careful step forward, his hands raised in a gesture of peace. "You must be going blind, old man. You don't even recognise the son of Jahlan Sword-Hand?"

Banu's eyes narrowed, flickering between recognition and disbelief. His grip tightened on the sword's hilt, then slowly loosened as memories pushed through the haze of suspicion.

"By the gods, we all thought you were dead!" Banu exclaimed, the edge of steel lowering but not disappearing.

Tareq nodded, giving a wide grin that was all too common across his face. "It takes more than a little fire to stop the Stags."

Banu finally sheathed his blade with a deliberate motion, approached Tareq and took him in a tight embrace. "Come. There is much to say, and time is short."

"I'm sorry to interrupt your reunion," she said, her tone steady but respectful. Her eyes moved from Banu to the rest of the gathered fighters, then back to her companions. "But they all need to hear what happened in the Blackhold."

Daran shifted his weight, glancing at Tareq, then back at the group. "There's not much to tell," he said quietly, the memory still raw in his voice.

Tareq gave a small nod, the faint light catching the deep lines and burns on his face. "We endured things in there that should never be spoken of, but you need to know... You need to understand what we're fighting against."

The campfire's crackle filled the silence that followed. Rebels gathered closer, their breath clouding in the cool air, eyes fixed on the two men as if the truth of the Blackhold might harden their resolve or break their spirits entirely.

Anya stepped back, letting Daran and Tareq move to the fire's edge, their faces half-lit in the orange glow. She folded her arms across her chest, watching them, her jaw tight. She knew the horrors they were about to share would wound every person here, the same way they had wounded her on their journey from the Blackhold.

Tareq stepped closer to the fire, his shadow stretching across the faces of those gathered. "We entered through the causeway," he began, his voice carrying just enough for the circle to hear. "The place was filled with other prisoners and magisters guards. They didn't speak. They didn't need to. Every one of them obeyed the magi without hesitation."

Daran's eyes were fixed on the flames as he took over. "The deeper we went, the colder it became. No torches, no lanterns, only a pale glow from the stones in the walls. They pulsed, like... like they were breathing."

Murmurs rippled through the rebels, but Anya raised a hand to silence them.

"They had prisoners," Daran continued, his jaw tightening. "Not in cells, not chained. They stood in rows, still and silent, their eyes clouded over. And every so often, one of them would move when a magister passed, like they were being pulled by strings." He looked down at the ground, unable to meet the eyes of any gathered there.

Tareq swallowed hard. "The magisters spoke in hushed voices about trying to keep the breach closed."

An uneasy silence fell over the camp.

"They took us to Cell Block Seven," Tareq said, his voice low but sharp. "It was not a prison… It was a workshop."

A few of the rebels shifted uncomfortably.

"They experimented on us," Tareq continued. "With elemental essence. They filled us with different alchemical mixtures to try to make our bodies strong enough to support it. With needles, with masks, sometimes just by pressing their hands to someone's chest and letting the energy pour in. They didn't care about us, just the results. Fire essence would crawl under the skin, blistering from the inside out." Tareq unconsciously touched the burns on his face.

Tareq's face tightened. "We heard them speak of another one, somewhere else in the Blackhold. But they talked about it as though it were more valuable than any other prisoner in Cell Block Seven."

One of the nearby prisoners trembled, trying to contain their tears.

The campfire popped loudly in the silence that followed. The rebels listened, the weight of the words sinking in. Each of them knew, deep down, that if the magisters could do such things once, they would do them again, and next time, it could be any of them.

Tareq's gaze fell to the dirt as he spoke again. "Once they realised the essence took hold, it didn't end. They called it the second phase…"

Tareq's voice was quieter now. "They told us the essence would tear us apart if we fought it. And they were right. You could feel it building, like heat under the skin or ice in the blood, pushing to be released. I…"

"That's enough," Daran interrupted, placing his hand on Tareq's shoulder.

The gathered rebels exchanged uneasy glances. The firelight played across their faces, some tight with suspicion, others with curiosity. Even in the relative safety of the camp, trust was a rare commodity.

Anya moved to stand between Tareq and Daran, and the rest of the gathering. "You've heard their account," she said, her voice carrying the authority of one used to command. "The magisters are not just killing our people. They are twisting them. Turning them into weapons. If these two survived with their minds intact, then they are proof of what we are truly fighting against."

Ula stepped forward, her pale eyes appearing completely white in the firelight. "If they kept speaking about another successful experiment..." she paused, clearly uneasy, "then there are more like them..."

Tareq nodded grimly. "We believe so. And if they still have the magi's leash around their necks, then they could be unleashed at any time."

Haldic, having listened to all that had been said so far, interrupted. "So, what do you propose? March to High Tower and ask politely for them to stop?"

"No," Anya said, her tone sharp enough to cut the tension. "We use what we learned in the Blackhold. We hit them where they least expect it. We continue gathering allies. We disrupt their supply lines. We weaken their hold until we can strike their next stronghold with purpose."

The rebels murmured among themselves, but Anya silenced them with a raised hand. "We plan carefully. We cannot afford to fail. The magisters may have lost one of their fortresses, but their power still reaches far."

A young rebel leaned forward eagerly. "If we can find and free those still held captive before they break them..."

"We will," Anya interrupted. "But we must be patient and precise."

Tareq and Daran exchanged a look. Both understood the weight of that statement all too well.

Anya then turned, her voice clear and steady as the camp fell silent around her. She looked out at the gathered freed prisoners, their faces marked by hardship, fear, and hope.

"You are free," she said, each word carrying the weight of promise. "The chains that bound you have been broken. Here, you will find safety, shelter, and the chance to heal."

She paused, scanning the crowd, making sure her message reached every ear.

"You may choose to return to your old lives, to your families and homes, if those remain. Or you may choose to stay and join us. Together, we fight to end the magisters' cruelty for all."

Anya's gaze softened, but her resolve remained firm. "Whatever you decide, there will be no judgement. For now, rest, recover. Gather your strength. The choice is yours when you are ready."

Murmurs rippled through the group. Some faces showed relief, others uncertainty. But in that moment, the spark of freedom kindled a fragile hope.

Nearby, Valdek and Banu moved among the people, offering quiet words of comfort and aid. Anya knew the road ahead would be long and hard, but this was the first step. A chance to rebuild.

Anya turned back to her gathered leaders, her voice calm but firm. "It has been a long few days. We need to rest and regroup before moving forward."

She let her gaze travel over the circle of faces, the weight of their
expectations pressing down. For a moment she faltered, her words trailing off
as though she had finished. Then her eyes found Haldic. The pause stretched
just long enough to betray her hesitation before she steadied herself.

"Join me in my tent," she said at last, her tone measured. "There is
something important I want to discuss."

Haldic shook his head, his eyes darted toward the darkened perimeter of the
camp. "Not tonight. I... I need to check on the eastern watch before the night
grows too deep. Make sure nothing slips past us." There was hesitation in his
gaze. A momentary glance toward the shadows beyond the camp, a tension in
his shoulders, the faint bite of unease in his voice.

A flash of hurt crossed Anya's face, though she masked it quickly. "Of
course. Be careful," she said, her voice steadier than she felt.

Haldic hesitated a fraction longer, his fingers brushing the hilt of his sword.
He swallowed, eyes flicking past her, and for a heartbeat his expression was
unreadable, tight around the edges. Then he nodded, turning toward the tents at
the edge of the camp with a quick, purposeful step.

As the flap fell shut behind her, Anya's shoulders sagged. The weight of
leadership pressed in, heavier now, and a subtle unease coiled in her chest.
Something about Haldic had felt... off. A stiffness in his movements, the way
he avoided her gaze, the way his eyes kept flicking toward the shadows. She

shook the thought away, telling herself it was just fatigue. Despite that, a quiet,

restless doubt lingered, gnawing at the back of her mind.

Chapter Eight

Weeks passed since the prisoners were freed from the Blackhold. The camp had transformed from a weary refuge into a bustling hub of resistance. Many of the former captives had chosen to stay, their spirits rekindled by the chance to fight for something greater than survival. They trained alongside seasoned rebels, learning to wield weapons, handle horses, and move silently through the forest. Others had made the hard decision to return to the ruins of their old homes, determined to rebuild whatever they could salvage of their former lives.

The camp echoed with new energy. Morning drills rang out across the clearing, mingling with the steady hammering of the forge. The smell of smoke and hot metal blended with the fresh pine air.

Daran was at the heart of this transformation. He had taken over the camp's forge, the place where broken weapons and armour came to be reborn. Day and night, he worked tirelessly, shaping steel and earthen elements into blades, shields, and armour. The flickering of the forge illuminated his focused expression as he repaired what was needed, knowing that each weapon handed out was another chance at victory and survival for the rebellion.

Nearby, Tareq practiced harnessing his flames, pushing the limits of control and endurance. His presence inspired the newer recruits, a living example of what the magisters' torture and experiments had failed to break.

As night fell and the camp quieted, the glow from the forge continued to burn bright, a symbol of hope and defiance in a land shadowed by oppression.

***

The forge's heat bled into the camp's cool evening air. Sparks leapt as Daran struck the final blows, shaping a mask that gleamed silver-brown in the firelight. It was made to cover the burned left side of Tareq's face, shaped to the contours of his ruined eye. A narrow slit remained for his good eye, sharp and watchful, and a larger gap at the mouth allowed for his familiar smile. Despite its sturdy make, the mask was light and balanced, moving easily with Tareq's expressions. Daran had shaped it to feel like a second skin, resilient to the touch, yet comfortable for long wear. Wiping the sweat from his brow, Daran stepped back and called out, "Tareq, come take a look at this."

Tareq approached cautiously, the flickering light reflecting in his one good eye. His gaze lingered on the mask, eyes tracing the delicate craftsmanship and the subtle glow of the earthen steel that blended strength with elegance.

"This is for you," Daran said quietly, voice steady but filled with something deeper. "To protect you out there, to remind you of everything we have been through..."

Tareq's gaze softened for a moment, gratitude and something harder to name flickering across his features. He reached out, running his fingers over the fine lines of the mask, reminiscent of how his face once was. He nodded slowly, his fingers brushing over the cold metal as if feeling the strength it promised.

Carefully, he lifted the mask to his face, feeling the cool surface settle against his skin, the edges fitting snugly around the burned flesh. It was heavier than he expected but somehow comforting. The metal helped ease the ache of his burns.

For the first time since the fire that had taken so much from him, Tareq felt a spark of something new. Not just anger, but of kinship.

Daran stepped closer, a faint smile tugging at the corners of his mouth. "Let me know if it doesn't fit right or needs adjusting," he mumbled. "I had to eyeball it since you weren't here, but I did my best."

Tareq reached out and pushed a small makeshift anvil aside, then clasped Daran's forearm, pulling him closer. Without a word, he leaned forward and pressed his forehead against Daran's.

Daran held the moment, his own breath steadying as he returned the unspoken promise.

Tareq pulled back slightly, a small smile playing on his lips as he looked at Daran. "Some others in the camp told me that's how your people show appreciation," he said. "Pressing foreheads, sharing a quiet moment. They said it means a lot."

Daran nodded, the faint smile still there. "It's a way to say we're in this together. There's no need for words."

For a brief moment, the weight of their shared past felt lighter. They were no longer just survivors, they were brothers-in-arms.

***

A Shatter Tooth scout staggered into camp, her horse collapsing in a wheeze of foam and dust at the edge of the fires. Smoke curled faintly from a singed cloak, the sharp stink of scorched fabric clinging to her as she pushed forward on trembling legs. Her pale eyes, wide and frantic, darted through the crowd until they locked on the tent at the camp's centre.

"Ula! Tsarevna!" she cried, her voice raw from the ride.

The rebels pointed, and she forced her way through, shoving aside shoulders with more desperation than strength. Ula and Anya had just stepped out when the scout fell before them, still gasping for breath.

"They're coming," she rasped, lowering her voice but not its edge. "The magi forces… They're close, burning their way through the northern hills. They've found us. We have little time."

A tense silence spread through the camp, the crackle of fire and idle chatter snuffed out at once. The only sound was the scout's ragged breathing.

Ula's pale eyes hardened, her hand tightening on the haft of her hooked blade. Beside her, Anya's jaw clenched, fingers curling around the hilt of her rapier.

"How far?" Anya demanded, her tone sharp.

The scout swallowed, chest still heaving. "A day, maybe two. They are pushing hard, but the hills will slow them, but not enough."

Anya turned to her captains. "Where should we regroup?"

Banu stepped forward. "We hold the high ground at the Ridge of Thorns. The narrow paths will slow their advance."

Haldic shook his head. "Too exposed. We should fall back to the old fortress ruins east of here. It offers better shelter and room to gather forces."

Valdek stepped in, his tone firm. "Both options leave us vulnerable. We need something stronger, more secure."

Before Anya could respond, Daran approached the nearby map and pointed with steady certainty. "The Ironjaw Gate," he said simply. "A mountain pass far to the south, on the border of Kul Vazhen. It is well guarded and almost impossible to bypass without being seen."

The leaders exchanged looks, weighing the suggestion. It was a dangerous choice, but it might be their best hope.

Anya's gaze settled firmly on Valdek. "You take over the planning. You know the logistics of moving our forces better than any."

Valdek stepped forward, his calm authority settling over the gathered captains like a steadying hand. His eyes scanned the map once more before turning to address the group.

"Our forces cannot move as one large body. We must divide into smaller, more agile groups and scatter across different routes," he explained. "This will confuse the Protectorate, making it harder for them to track or trap us. Our goal remains clear. We make our way south toward the Ironjaw Gate."

He paused, letting the weight of his words sink in.

"Along the way, we must strike swiftly and decisively against any patrols we encounter," Valdek continued. "Free prisoners, disrupt supply lines, and recruit those who are willing to join our cause. Each new ally strengthens us."

His voice hardened with resolve. "We will need to gather every bit of food, weapons, and armour we can find. Supplies are just as vital as bodies in this fight. Our survival depends on your resourcefulness as much as strength."

Anya nodded, a flicker of pride in her tired eyes. "Good. Move swiftly but carefully. We cannot afford mistakes. The rebellion's future rests on this journey."

The captains exchanged determined glances, some already calculating routes and resources.

Haldic stepped forward, his tone measured but firm. "I understand the reasoning behind splitting up," he said, "but moving as one strong force has its advantages. The magisters will expect us to scatter. They will prepare for that."

He looked around the group. "If we travel together, our combined strength could overwhelm any opposition. It will send a clear message that we are no longer scattered rebels but a unified force to be reckoned with."

His eyes locked with Valdek's. "Splitting up risks leaving isolated groups vulnerable. The magisters are cunning. They will exploit any weakness."

Valdek met the challenge steadily, his voice calm but edged with conviction. "Travelling as one large force might look impressive, but it will almost certainly lead to our capture or destruction. The magisters have greater numbers, greater resources. To march as a single body is to walk straight into their trap."

He shook his head slowly. "Such a strategy would be arrogant and short-sighted."

Haldic's jaw clenched, eyes flashing. "Short-sighted?" His voice rose like a blade striking steel. "You dare insult my judgment and experience? Your words drip with conceit, not wisdom."

He stepped closer, stabbing a finger at the map spread across the table. "Strength in unity is not reckless, it is our only weapon. Divide us, and this rebellion dies piece by piece."

The air thickened. Several leaders shifted in their seats, some murmuring agreement with Haldic, others with Valdek. Hands rested uneasily on hilts. The crackle of the fire seemed to fade beneath the sharp silence of a room on the verge of breaking.

Valdek's voice hardened, though he kept his composure. "I do not question your courage, Captain Haldic, but courage without caution is nothing but a death wish. We must survive by being cunning, not by charging headlong into the magisters' jaws."

The tent pulsed with tension, every man and woman inside caught between the two arguments. Anya felt conflicted by the wisdom of her oldest friend, and her feelings towards Haldic.

Haldic's anger burned so close to the surface she could almost feel its heat, and she knew siding with Valdek now would drive the sting deeper. Yet to waver would fracture her command before it had the chance to be whole.

She stepped forward, raising her hand, her voice cutting through the rising clash. "Enough." Her voice was firm, although inside her chest, her heart hammered. "Both of you speak truth, drawn from hard-earned scars. But right now, we must trust Valdek's plan. It offers us the best chance to endure."

Her gaze lingered on Haldic, willing him to bend without breaking. He glared back at her, his pride wounded, but after a long moment he gave a stiff nod. The fire in his eyes dimmed, but it did not die.

***

As the camp buzzed with hurried activity, tents were struck down, and supplies packed quickly into wagons. The air was thick with urgency and tension, the sounds of murmured orders and clinking metal filling the space. Tareq and Daran moved through the press with purpose until they found Anya at the camp's edge, overseeing the last of the preparations.

They drew her aside, far enough from the others to speak in private.

Daran broke the silence first, his voice low but steady. "We need to talk. It's about the road ahead."

Anya turned to them, sensing the weight in his tone.

Tareq took a slow breath. "We've thought this through. The magi will come for us over anyone else. If we stay with you, we put everyone in greater danger." His gaze met hers, steady but grim. "The Protectorate will strike with everything they have."

Daran stepped in, resolute. "If we move separately, we can draw their eyes away from the rebellion. We'll take another path and meet you in Kul Vazhen."

Anya's chest tightened. For a moment she wanted to argue, to forbid it, to tell them she needed them at her side. But she saw the decision was already settled on their faces. To fight it would only waste what little time remained.

She steadied her voice, though a flicker of dread pulsed beneath. "If this is what you believe is best, then I will trust your judgment. But be cautious. The road will be dangerous… and I won't forgive you if you don't come back."

Daran gave a firm nod. "We'll see you at the Ironjaw."

Tareq's voice was quieter, almost gentle. "We'll keep our heads down. You'll see us again."

For a heartbeat, none of them moved, the moment stretched on with unspoken fear and trust. Then, with a final glance that carried more weight than words could hold, Tareq and Daran turned and slipped into the dusk, vanishing into the shadows of the dismantling camp.

Chapter Nine

The road south was long and quiet, save for the crunch of boots on dirt and the faint rasp of Tareq's swords against their sheaths. Ash still carried on the wind, curling from the west, and every step away from the rebellion's camp felt heavier than the last.

Ahead, the silence broke. A cart lay across the road, one wheel snapped clean through, its axle sagging like a broken bone. An old man in faded green robes knelt beside it, fumbling with the spokes. His hair was white, his hands shaking as he struggled alone. No guards, no soldiers. Just a swaybacked mule, restless and stamping at flies.

Tareq stiffened, fire already itching at his fingertips. "A magister."

Daran grunted, his hand resting on the haft of his hammer but not lifting it. "Not much of one left, by the look of him."

Tareq drew his swords and started towards the magister.

The man turned at their voices. His eyes widened with fear, and he fell backwards onto the ground. He lifted a trembling hand, palm outward. "Please," he croaked. "I mean you no harm. Only… the cart. The wheel won't hold any longer, but I must reach the other villages."

Tareq barked a sharp laugh. "To bleed them dry, or to take their children?"

The magister shook his head. "No, not that. I was never one for fighting. I studied herbs, both root and leaf, making cures. When the Protectorate came, I thought I could do more good with their help. I make tinctures for fever, balms for the lungs. The villages beyond the pass are ill. If I can't get these supplies to them…" His shoulders sagged.

He gestured to the back of the cart. Bundles of herbs and jars of ground powders lay neatly packed, smelling faintly of mint and resin, not rot and metal.

Daran crouched to inspect the wheel. "Cracked through the axle. You won't fix this alone." He glanced at the old man.

The magister nodded, fumbling with a wrapped bundle. "I can give you food if you help, fresh bread and salted meat. A hearty meal for strong arms. And…" His gaze lingered on Tareq, on the scars visible beneath his mask that crawled from jaw to collar. "An ointment for burns. It will help ease the pain. Not a cure, but… it may grant you rest."

For a heartbeat, neither man moved. Tareq's fire licked faintly at his palm before he smothered it. His voice was sharp, but not as sure. "And why should I trust anything a magister gives me?"

The old man met his eyes, voice shaking but steady. "Because lies waste time I don't have. And because not all of us sought power. Some of us only wanted to heal."

The words hung in the air. Tareq's fire guttered but didn't vanish. He sneered, though softer this time. "And yet you wore their colours, you called them master."

The magister looked down, the shame was heavy on his face. "I did... I do. But regret doesn't heal the sick and injured. All I can do is tend the living."

The silence stretched. Daran exhaled and set to work. He braced the axle, hammered a dowel into place, and soon the wheel was fitted again. The old man watched, relief lining his weary face.

"You've done more for me than others of my order ever would. Thank you." He pressed the bundle of food into Daran's hands, and a small jar into Tareq's. The thick liquid inside was pale green, and smelled faintly of sage and smoke. "For the nights when the scars burn the most."

Tareq hesitated and then took it without a word and put it in his satchel.

When the mule had pulled the cart away, Daran spoke. "Strange road we walk. Magisters who heal instead of harm."

Tareq spat into the dust, but the motion felt hollow. "Or maybe it's the cruellest trick yet. To make us think some of them cared."

Yet as the cart vanished around the bend, his hand brushed the jar in his bag.

***

That night, they camped beneath a broken arch of stone, the fire low and mean against the creeping dark. Daran was already snoring softly when Tareq pulled the jar from his bag. The ointment caught the firelight, green and gold, almost alive. His hand trembled as he uncorked it.

It could be poison. It could be another trick.

But the scars across his chest, arm and face were burning worse than the flames in his veins. Sleep had been a stranger for a long time.

He slowly rubbed it into his scars.

It was thick and oily, but within moments the pain dulled. His jaw loosened. For the first time in years, his body felt his own again. He slumped against the stone, eyes closing in a haze of warmth and relief.

When sleep finally claimed him, it wasn't filled with screams.

***

The next morning, Daran crouched by the fire, stirring a pan of oats. He looked up as Tareq stretched and sat up, blinking the sleep from his eyes.

"You slept," Daran said, voice tinged with surprise.

Tareq gave a half-smile. "What of it?"

"You haven't slept straight through since... well, ever." Daran leaned closer, squinting at the scars across Tareq's body. "And your burns... they don't look as angry."

Tareq hesitated, then reached for his satchel. But Daran caught the movement and raised a brow. "What did you do?"

Reluctantly, Tareq pulled the small glass jar from his bag.

Daran's brows rose higher. "The magister gave that to you."

Tareq sighed, almost defensively. "It worked for a while... I can feel it wearing off."

Daran studied him for a long moment, then sat back on his heels, the surprise still clear on his face. "I just never thought I'd see you take something from one of them."

Tareq's voice was quiet, but steady. "You think I don't remember what they did? Every scar reminds me. But that old man wasn't like the others. If even one of them was truly trying to help, then maybe… maybe things aren't as simple as we want them to be."

Daran didn't answer right away. He stirred the oats again, slow and thoughtful, his eyes flicking to the jar.

"Maybe," he said at last, softly. "Or maybe that's how they win, by making us believe they're not all the same."

The words hung between them, not sharp, but heavy. Tareq tucked the jar away again, his jaw set, and neither man spoke as the fire cracked softly in the silence.

Chapter Ten

Several months had slipped by since they had left the northern camp behind. The journey had been long, with harsh weather and relentless danger pressing in at every turn. Now, finally, the jagged mountains marking the border of Kul Vazhen rose ahead, their dark, craggy peaks standing like silent sentinels against the pale morning sky. Far in the distance, the Ironjaw Gate carved a narrow path through the stone, a looming gateway that promised both hope and peril.

Tareq swung down from his horse with practiced ease, the weight of the journey clear in his movements. Near a small stream that wound its way through the rocky earth, he eased the reins from the tired animal's neck. The horse lowered its head eagerly, drinking deeply from the cold water.

Reaching into the worn leather saddlebag, Tareq pulled out a strip of dried meat. He tore off a bite, chewing slowly as he allowed the moment's quiet to settle around them. The steady babble of the stream and the whisper of wind through the trees were the only sounds breaking the heavy silence that stretched between the two men.

"We're almost there," Tareq finally said, his voice low but firm. His eyes rested on the distant silhouette of the Ironjaw Gate, a faint glimmer of hope in an otherwise grim journey.

Daran stood nearby, sitting on a fallen tree. His gaze was fixed on that same distant gate, though his expression was unreadable. He had spoken very little over the course of their long travels, through rain and snow, or the weight of endless threats and close battles. His silence carried a heavy burden, thick with memories of loss, pain, and the desperate hope that had driven them onward.

Tareq watched him carefully, sensing the storm of thoughts swirling behind those quiet, guarded eyes. He knew Daran carried more than just the scars of battle and the torture they endured. There were wounds deeper still.

For a long moment, neither of them spoke. A gust of cold mountain wind stirred the surface of the stream. The world around them seemed to hold its breath, waiting for what would come next.

"Why do you always smile?" Daran muttered, "No matter how bad it gets."

Tareq chuckled. "My father once said, 'Never let your enemies know how you feel, never show them that you're hurting. Sometimes that alone is enough to win the fight.' And I guess it just stuck with me."

The silence grew again. Then, slowly, Daran nodded.

"Fathers and their wisdom," he said with a wry smile. "Mine told me once that most folk don't get to choose who they work beside. But..." He let the thought hang heavily in the air before finishing. "I'm glad I've got you beside me, Tareq."

A grin rarely left Tareq's face, although this time there was a flicker of warmth behind it. Finally, Tareq broke the silence once more. "Whatever lies ahead, we'll face it together. You're not alone."

Daran met his gaze.

***

As Tareq and Daran pressed onward toward the Ironjaw Gate, the towering cliffs on either side of the narrow pass seemed to close in around them. The air grew colder, carrying the faint scent of ground earth. The heavy weight of their journey was settling into their bones, but the faint outline of the gate ahead promised relief. A passage to safety, or at least into the next phase of their struggle.

Suddenly, a sharp, commanding voice rang out from high above on the ramparts.

"Hold where you are! Identify yourselves!"

The words sliced through the quiet mountain air, halting them instantly.

Figures emerged along the battlements, their forms silhouetted against the pale sky. Men and women, grim-faced and alert, stood ready with weapons drawn. A mixture of bows and crossbows gleamed in their hands, strings pulled taut and aimed directly at the two approaching riders.

Arrows and bolts rested on notched strings, poised to fly at the slightest provocation. The cold steel tips caught the light and sent a clear and deadly message.

Then Tareq spotted the banners fluttering behind the guards. The familiar sigils of the rebellion. His eyes narrowed with recognition. These were not enemies but sentries on high alert, unsure of who approached their stronghold.

"Lower your bloody weapons!" Tareq called out, voice steady and commanding. "Don't you recognise us?"

A moment passed, tense and watchful, before a few arrows and bolts slowly lowered, followed by others. The stringed weapons settled down as the guards relaxed their grip, though their eyes remained sharp.

Tareq then raised his hand toward one torch blazing atop the wall. With a controlled motion, he summoned a ribbon of fire from the flame, drawing it upward in a graceful arc, and gave a large grin. The glowing trail caught the attention of those above, a sure sign of who he was.

As the portcullis raised, Tareq and Daran exchanged a glance. Although their journey was over, it was only the beginning.

***

Anya burst out into the courtyard just as the massive gates groaned shut, her breath coming quick with a mix of relief and anticipation. Without a second thought, she closed the distance between herself and the two riders, pulling Tareq and Daran into a fierce, almost desperate embrace. Her arms wrapped tightly around them, grounding herself in the solid presence of the friends she feared she had lost.

"What took you so long?" she asked, her voice trembling slightly with a mixture of worry and frustration. Her eyes searched their faces, looking for any sign of injury or worse.

Tareq's lips curved into a tired but proud smile as he gently patted her back. "We did what we could," he said quietly, his voice rough from the long journey and countless battles. "We made sure the magisters paid for every step they took on our land. We hurt them as much as possible on the way down here."

Daran stood close, exhaustion etched deep in his features. His gaze was steady, though weary, as if carrying the weight of all they had endured. He said nothing, but the look in his eyes told everything, a promise to keep fighting, no matter the cost.

Anya pulled back slightly, resting her forehead against Tareq's shoulder for a moment. "That's what I needed to hear," she whispered. Then, realising that everyone was watching them, she straightened and took a step back, looking both of them in the eyes.

"We have no time to waste. It won't take the magisters long to find out where we are. We need to continue strengthening our forces, tend to the wounded, and prepare for what comes next."

Together, the three of them turned toward the heart of the rebel camp. The sun was setting behind the jagged mountain peaks, casting long shadows across the buildings and thick stone walls.

***

The next morning, as the pale light filtered through the fort, Daran found Tareq near the forge where the steady ring of hammer against metal filled the air. The camp was waking, but their conversation needed quiet, away from prying eyes and ears.

Daran's voice was low and steady but carried a weight that made Tareq stop mid-motion. "There's something I need to do," he said, glancing briefly toward the southern horizon. "In a village to the south."

Tareq's eyes narrowed with concern, stepping closer without hesitation. "Let me get my swords," he said firmly.

Daran shook his head with quiet resolve, his jaw tightening. "No. This is something I need to do by myself." He looked directly at Tareq, the determination in his gaze unwavering.

Tareq hesitated, the urge to insist conflicting with his respect for Daran's wishes. He finally nodded, though the worry in his eyes remained. "Just be careful," he said, placing a firm hand on Daran's shoulder. "Whatever it is, we'll be here when you return. You're not alone."

A small, grateful smile touched Daran's lips. "Thank you, Tareq."

With that, Daran turned toward the southern gate of the keep, already plotting his course and steeling himself for the journey ahead. Tareq watched him go, the weight of the coming days settling between them.

***

As Daran entered his old village, the sights and sounds stirred a quiet storm inside him. The streets he once knew so well stretched out before him, unchanged in their crooked charm, yet wrapped in a heavy silence that seemed to weigh the very air down. Where once laughter and the clatter of daily life had filled the air, now only the faint rustling of wind through barren trees answered his presence.

The cobblestones beneath his horse's hooves, once stained dark with blood and ash from a terrible past, had been scrubbed clean, as if the village itself had tried to bury its wounds. The houses, though weathered by time, stood stubbornly upright, their walls bearing the marks of years but hiding the scars of old pain.

As he rode slowly through the village, memories flooded him. The warmth of Ora's smile, the quiet moments shared beneath the stars, the laughter of children playing near the well. But those moments felt distant, like a dream fading at dawn.

When he reached Ora's old house, Daran felt his heart tighten. The small wooden door, rough-hewn and simple, looked just as it had all those years ago. A thin wisp of smoke curled from the chimney, and the scent of earth and wood lingered faintly on the air.

Daran dismounted carefully, each movement deliberate as if trying not to disturb the fragile calm. He approached the door with measured steps. His hand trembled as he raised it, and his knuckles rapped against the weathered wood. Three slow, steady knocks that echoed softly in the stillness.

For a moment, there was no answer. The silence stretched, heavy and expectant. Footsteps, cautious and slow, started to sound somewhere past the door. The door creaked open just a crack, and the dark face of an elderly woman appeared in the narrow gap. Daran's voice dropped low as he said her name, "Siku." He recognised her immediately as Ora's mother.

His heart tightened, and he struggled to find the right words. "Siku, I am so sorry. For everything that happened. For not being there. I never wanted this to come to this."

Siku's eyes filled with tears, and a shaky breath escaped her lips. Her shoulders shook as she fought back sobs. After a moment, she whispered, "Ora... she waits by the large oak on the edge of the village."

Daran felt a sharp pang in his chest. Before he could say anything more, Siku closed the door with a heavy slam, leaving him alone in the quiet street. The silence pressed down around him, thick with grief and hope.

***

Daran moved slowly toward the large oak at the edge of the village. The surrounding ground was a sombre sea of simple grave markers. Rough, weathered stones standing unevenly like forgotten sentinels. Each one bore silent testimony to those who had perished at the hands of the magisters. The wind whispered through the branches above, carrying the hollow weight of loss across the barren fields.

His eyes searched the worn names and dates carved crudely into the stones until they finally settled on a small, plain marker.

Ora's grave.

It was unpolished and roughly hewn, the work of unskilled hands. The master craftsmen who once shaped elegant tombstones had long since been taken by the magisters. All that remained was this humble token of a life unjustly cut short before it's time.

Daran's breath caught. His legs trembled beneath him and then finally gave way. He sank to his knees before the grave, the rough earth cold and unforgiving beneath him. The silence pressed in, broken only by the soft rustling of leaves overhead and the faint crackle of dried grass underfoot.

For a long moment, he could do nothing but stare. His throat tightened, and a lump formed, choking back words. What felt like a lifetime of pain, regret, and grief he had carried with him. Bottled up and buried deep inside, it broke free in a torrent. Tears streamed down his face, carving tracks through the grime and dust. His hands clenched the earth at the base of the stone, knuckles white with the force of his silent anguish.

He wanted to scream, to curse the cruel fate that had taken her from him, but no sound came. Instead, the grief poured out in the quietest way possible, through trembling shoulders, ragged breaths, and the steady fall of tears onto the cold stone.

In that moment, Daran allowed himself to feel the full weight of his loss. All the fighting, running, and surviving felt distant and hollow compared to the ache in his chest. For the first time in a long time, he let his sorrow claim him, seeking release in the graveyard's stillness beneath the ancient oak.

Daran slowly lowered his hand to the earth in front of Ora's grave. The cold, rough soil pressed against the metal and stone of his fingers, grounding him in the moment. He closed his eyes, reaching deep into his memory, calling forth every detail of her face. The gentle curve of her smile, the fierce light that always danced in her eyes, the way her dark hair caught the sunlight, soft and flowing, when it wasn't bound tightly in braids.

He drew a steady breath and focused his will. The earth essence was faint, but still pulsed within him, responding to his call. His muscles tightened beneath worn clothes, his chest rising and falling in a measured rhythm. Slowly, almost hesitantly, his stone hand glowed with a subtle brown light, mirroring the earthen steel's faint sheen.

With a mighty strain, he pushed upward, feeling the ground beneath tremble and shift. Cracks splintered across the soil and flagstones around the grave as chunks of rock and earth loosened, rising in a swirling, spiralling pillar. The pillar grew taller and taller, raw stone swirling upward as if breathed to life by his determination.

Shapes took form within the rising column. The jagged edges smoothing into the graceful curves of a woman's figure. The rough stone softened, carving itself into delicate features, with the likeness of Ora emerging in stunning detail. Her face was serene yet strong, etched with the memory of a soul that had never truly left.

Where once a simple, weathered gravestone stood, now there was a statue. The stone shimmered faintly with the same subtle brown tinge that marked Daran's hand, as a quiet reminder of the earth essence that bound them. The statue stood tall beneath the ancient oak, a sentinel of memory and love.

Daran's breath calmed as he gently lowered his hand. With the pillar settled into place, the earth beneath was unwavering. He knelt before the statue, the weight of years pressing down but tempered by the presence of the form before him. For a long moment, silence stretched between them, broken only by the rustle of wind through the oak's leaves.

In the stillness, Daran felt something stir. A fragile hope, a tether to the past, and a strength to face what lay ahead. Ora's memory, now carved in stone and earth, was more than a monument. It was a promise. It was a reminder that even with everything that had been lost, life could endure, and from the ashes of sorrow, something new and beautiful could grow.

***

Daran's footsteps echoed softly across the empty village street as he made his way toward the ruins of his father's old forge. The building stood battered and broken, its wooden beams splintered, the roof partially caved in. Time and neglect had claimed what no enemy ever could. The villagers had long abandoned the place, lacking both the skill and the will to revive the heart of their craftsmanship.

He approached the ruin. His gaze fixed on the scattered stones and twisted metal. Without hesitation, Daran dropped to his knees and sifted through the debris. Dust coated his hands as he brushed aside broken bricks and shattered tiles, searching for something that would still connect him to his father.

Beneath a fallen anvil, half-buried in the earth, his fingers closed around the familiar haft of a hammer. It was his hammer. Worn and scarred from use, still bearing the blood of one of the magister guards, it remained unbroken. The weight of it felt like a lifeline in his palm, connecting him to the past and to the father who had helped shape the tool and the man he had become.

Daran's fingers lingered on the cool metal of the hammer as he stood amidst the wreckage. The familiar weight grounded him, stirring a storm of memories. The rhythm of the forge's fires, the steady clang of hammer against anvil, his father's patient voice guiding his hands through each strike. Here in this ruined village, those moments seemed like echoes from another life, distant and fragile.

Around him, the village lay silent and empty. Windows stared back like hollow eyes, their shutters hanging askew. This was once a place of warmth and industry, where families lived and dreams were forged in metal and fire. Now it was a ghost of that past, a testament to everything taken from them.

Daran's gaze drifted to the horizon where the Ironjaw Gate waited, a stone sentinel carved into the rugged mountain pass. The weight on his heart was heavy, but the hammer at his side was a reminder that he still carried a piece of his father's strength within him.

He slid the hammer's handle into the worn leather loop on his belt, feeling a sense of resolve settle deep in his bones, and pulled the anvil upright, and placed his father's hammer that he took from the Blackhold carefully on top. Although not as elegant as the statue he made for Ora, he knew that this would resonate with his father's spirit. The cold wind whispered through the broken rooftops, ruffling his cloak, as if urging him onward. With one last look at the village, at the shattered forge, the empty streets, and the graves that told stories of sacrifice, Daran mounted his horse.

The animal shifted beneath him, muscles coiling and relaxing as it prepared to move. Daran took the reins in hand, eyes narrowing as he guided the horse northward, towards the Ironjaw Gate and the uncertain future beyond. Each step of the horse on the rough path was a beat of determination, a silent vow to carry the memory of those lost and to fight for a new dawn

Chapter Eleven

Daran pushed open the heavy southern gates of the Ironjaw and rode into the courtyard. The afternoon sun spilled over the stone walls, but the light did little to brighten the tense scene unfolding in the centre.

Daran dismounted slowly. The courtyard was thick with tension, every breath heavy as the air before lightning. The stone beneath his boots was cracked and worn, but the surrounding noise was alive. Weapons were drawn from their sheaths, voices raised in anger and the restless murmur of a crowd close to breaking.

At the centre stood Ula, her curved blade gleaming in the morning light, pressed to the throat of a captive lancer. The man at her feet was kneeling, sweat slicked his pale face, fear fighting against his soldier's drilled composure. His bound hands twitched helplessly as the knife bit lightly at his skin.

Haldic strode forward, voice firm but tight with anger. "Ula, release him. We must show strength, not cruelty. We hold the law here, not barbarity."

Ula's pale eyes burned cold. "He's a spy," she growled. "We caught him with letters that map our movements. His life is forfeit."

Shouts rippled through the gathered rebels. "Kill him now!" one bellowed, echoed by others. "Spare him and he'll slit our throats in the night!" someone else spat. Others pushed back. "And what then, when every village hears we butcher captives?" Voices rose and collided, sharp and furious.

A lancer shoved a Shatter Tooth, their blades flashed half-free. The courtyard bristled like a powder keg with the sparks already hissing toward the fuse.

Anya stepped out of the wall's shadow, her stomach tight with dread, though her face betrayed nothing. Her eyes flicked to the satchel at the lancer's side, battered but still intact. "If these letters speak truth, his capture may have saved lives. But if we act rashly, we risk losing every alliance we have left."

Her words did nothing to sate Ula's fury. Her grip on her knife tightened, the blade digging enough to draw a bead of blood. Haldic's hand went to his hilt. The gathered Shatter Tooth growled, shifting closer towards their leader, while lancers bristled in return.

Anya knew one heartbeat more would see the keep splinter in blood. She drew herself tall, her voice cracking like thunder over the clamour.

"Enough!"

The single word cut through the courtyard. Hands froze on their blades. Every breath was stilled. Dozens of eyes fixed on her. She stepped between captor and prisoner, one hand rested on her rapier's hilt, the other came to gently rest on Ula's arm.

Her voice rang clear, steady as the stone walls around them. "Yes, he may be a spy. Yes, betrayal stalks us in every shadow. But if we turn on each other now, the magisters win without lifting a single finger. Trust must be earned, and betrayal punished. But we must be just, or we are no better than the magisters themselves."

Her words silenced the gathered crowd. Ula eased her knife back a fraction, though her gaze remained as cold as the stone around them. Haldic released his hilt, jaw clenched. The prisoner sagged in terrified relief.

Banu's deep voice broke the stillness as he stepped forward, his dark eyes sweeping the crowd. "The lancers move far too often through these mountains for chance. This man is not the first, and he will not be the last. Watch the paths. Watch each other. The magi will strike soon."

The rebels slowly backed down, the storm contained, though the air was heavy with blood not yet spilled.

***

Anya's eyes found Daran as the courtyard slowly returned to normal, though the tension still hung thick in the air from Ula's accusations and Haldic's heated defence. The captive lancer remained on his knees, guarded closely by the Shatter Tooth warriors, and murmurs still rippled through the gathered rebels.

"Where have you been?" Anya demanded, stepping toward him. "Tareq told me nothing more than 'He'll be back' and continued about his business. I was left wondering if you'd been taken by the magisters... or if you had simply walked away. And now, of all times, you appear. Right in the middle of all this!"

Daran stood still, letting the sharpness of her words wash over him. His eyes flicked briefly to the captured lancer, then back to her. The smell of dust and smoke clung to him, his clothes still travel-stained, and there was something in his gaze that carried more weight than his voice could yet hold.

"There was something I needed to do," he said at last, low and deliberate. "It was my burden alone."

Anya's shoulders eased slightly as she let out a long sigh. "We've had enough mistrust and uncertainty today," she said, glancing toward the Shatter Tooth warrior who still had her blade poised. "Next time, don't vanish without a word. You're not alone, Daran."

Daran nodded once, saying nothing more, but the look in his eyes told her there was more to the story than he was ready to share.

***

The next morning, Anya was roused from her sleep by a firm knock at her door. Pulling on her coat against the chill, she opened it to find Valdek standing there with one of the Lancer captains, a reliable man named Marek. His shoulders were slumped, and his eyes avoided hers, as though bracing for the weight of his own words.

Valdek inclined his head in a quiet apology for the early hour, his tone low but urgent. "I'm sorry, Tsarevna, but this couldn't wait."

He then turned to Marek, giving a slight nod of encouragement.

Marek stepped forward reluctantly, his voice heavy with shame. "Captain Haldic is gone. He left sometime during the night."

Anya was about to question him, but Marek lifted a hand, pushing through. "The lancer caught yesterday by the Shatter Tooth was acting under Haldic's orders. He was carrying messages meant for the magisters."

The words struck like a blade between her ribs. For a moment, her composure cracked. The memory of Haldic's hand brushing her hair back, the warmth of his breath in the dark, the fire of their arguments giving way to something sharper, more intimate. Fury and pain surged hot in her chest, and she wanted to scream, to shatter the chair beside her against the wall, to deny the truth.

But she pushed it down. Her fists tightened at her sides, the chill of the morning biting deeper. When she spoke, her voice was sharp and controlled. "Do you know where he is heading?"

Marek shook his head. "I'm sorry, Tsarevna, no one knows. It's likely he's heading to a pre-arranged meeting place with a magister patrol, with detailed plans of everything that we're doing here."

Silence pressed heavily. Valdek's expression hardened as he turned to her. "We must decide quickly. The magisters will know our movements, our strengths and our weaknesses."

Deep within the keep, a raised voice carried through the stone halls. Ula, no doubt, was already demanding that they hunt Haldic down before he could reach his masters. The Ironjaw felt smaller than it had the day before, its thick walls no longer a shield but a trap.

Anya drew a long breath, forcing the tremor from her chest. She looked between them, her tone low but steady. "Wake the others. This changes everything."

***

The council gathered in the Ironjaw's great hall, the long table crowded with maps, candles, and tankards of untouched ale. The air was thick with the smell of wet stone and the low murmur of soldiers outside the doors, all waiting to hear what would be decided.

Anya sat at the head, her hands resting on the edge of the table, while Ula leaned against a pillar like a coiled spring, her eyes fixed on Marek. Banu sat with his arms crossed, his gaze sharp and distrustful, while Valdek stood just behind Anya's chair, silent and watchful.

Marek, still pale from the morning's revelations, cleared his throat. "There is... another matter," he began, his voice hesitant but firm enough to carry over the crackle of the hearth. "The lancers who remain here, my men, we were sworn to serve Captain Haldic, not the Tsarevna, or this rebellion. Our oath was to him alone."

The words landed like stones dropped into still water.

Anya's eyes narrowed. "And what does that mean, exactly?"

Marek shifted uncomfortably but did not look away. "It means our standing orders are clear. If Captain Haldic were to fall in battle or no longer hold command, we are to return to our lord's service without delay. Some are already questioning why we remain here now that he is gone."

Ula pushed off the pillar, her voice cold and sharp. "Then why are you still here? Waiting for him to come back? Or for the magi to send you your next orders?"

Marek bristled but held his ground. "I stayed because I believe in what we are doing here. Some of my men feel the same. But others…" He glanced down at the map, avoiding Banu's piercing stare. "…the others will not fight without their captain. They see this cause as no longer theirs."

Banu leaned forward, and spat into the fire, his voice a low growl. "Then we have a nest of deserters within our own walls!"

Anya's voice cut through before the argument could boil over. "Enough. If we turn on each other now, Haldic has won." She looked to Marek, her tone measured. "If you want to stay, you and your men will swear new oaths to me and to our cause, or you will leave before sundown. I will not have soldiers in my ranks who are unsure which way their sword points."

The silence that followed was tense, broken only by the wind rattling against the shutters. Marek nodded slowly. "I will speak to them. But you should be ready, not everyone will accept."

Ula smirked without humour. "Good. Less mouths to feed when the siege comes."

Valdek leaned forward, placing a fresh map on the table. "If Haldic reaches

the magisters with our plans, it will not matter how many lancers remain. We

will be fighting on their terms."

Anya leaned forward, pressing her palms against the table. "We have no time

to waste chasing shadows. Whether it's tomorrow or in a week, they will come

for us. We must prepare the Ironjaw for a siege."

Banu grunted in approval. "Then we start by filling the mountain pass with

debris, at least enough to slow them down and reduce the numbers they can

bring to us at a time."

Ula's pale eyes glinted. "And double the watches. I will have my hunters

patrol the high ridges. No one will slip through without being seen."

Valdek stepped forward, already thinking ahead. "We will need to bring

every scrap of food into the keep, reinforce the gates, and check the cisterns. If

we are trapped here, water will be more precious than steel."

Anya nodded once, then turned to Marek. "Speak to your men. I need to

know who will fight and who will walk away before we put our backs to the

wall. If they choose to leave, they leave today."

Marek straightened, his face still drawn but his voice steady. "I will speak to

them." He gave a shallow bow and turned, striding out of the hall without

another word.

The heavy doors closed behind him, and for a moment the only sound was the crackle of the hearth. Outside, the Ironjaw's courtyard bustled with the sounds of soldiers and mercenaries beginning to move at new orders.

Anya looked to the others. "This fort has stood against worse. It will continue to stand."

Banu's brow furrowed. "If your lancers stay."

Ula gave a sharp smile. "If they don't, we will just fill the walls with warriors who have no doubts about where their loyalty lies."

No one disagreed. The room emptied in pairs and trios, each leader heading out to oversee their own preparations, leaving Anya for a moment alone in the hall.

She stared at the great map of the valley on the table, its ink lines tracing mountains, rivers, and roads, wondering just how soon those roads would carry the magisters to her gates.

***

The chill morning air bit against Marek's cheeks as he stepped into the Ironjaw courtyard. The clang of hammers, the shuffle of boots on stone, and the distant shouts of orders echoed off the high walls. The lancers stood in a loose knot near the stables, their polished armour shined but their faces were shadowed with unease.

They straightened as he approached, though the movement was slow, hesitant. Marek could feel the question in the air before anyone spoke.

He stopped before them, his voice carrying clearly across the yard. "Haldic is gone." The murmurs started immediately, a ripple of disbelief and anger. Marek raised a hand, silencing them. "The magisters know the rebellion is here. The man caught yesterday was carrying letters for them, on Haldic's orders. There is no hiding the truth now."

One of the older sergeants stepped forward. "And what of us, sir? Our oath is to Haldic, not the Tsarevna."

Marek's jaw tightened. "Your oath is to defend those who cannot defend themselves. If you walk away now, you do so with the knowledge that the magisters will burn this valley, every farm and every family in it, just like they did in the western holds. If you stay, you will fight alongside men and women who will hold this fortress to the last."

A young lancer frowned. "And if Haldic returns?"

Marek met his eyes. "Then he will answer for what he has done. But if we falter now, there will be nothing left to return to."

For a moment, silence pressed in. Then the older sergeant spat on the stone. "I won't continue to bleed for her, not after this." He turned sharply, clapping a hand on the younger lancer's shoulder. The boy flinched under the weight of it, torn between duty and honour.

Before the sergeant could drag him away, Marek called out. "You, boy."

The youth froze, glancing back.

"If you leave, then let *Ksiaze* Sobieska know what's happened here. Tell him that most of his men broke. That they abandoned this fortress and those within it when they were needed most. Tell him that although they disobeyed his orders, some of his men held their ground against uncertain odds because it was the right thing to do, it was what their honour demanded. Tell him… Tell him that we who remain do so with pride."

The courtyard fell silent. The young lancer's throat bobbed as he swallowed, shame burning on his face. Finally, he gave a jerky nod.

The sergeant pulled him away, and the fracture spread like a crack in glass. Arguments broke out, voices raised, men shoved one another, torn between oath and what was just. Some cursed Marek openly, others shouted for the sergeant, until at last the group split apart. Nearly two dozen peeled away toward the southern gate, their mounts' hooves crunching hard against the frost, while a smaller handful lingered in bitter silence.

When the gate swung open, the deserters left in a ragged line, their spears carried high as though to make a point. Only three remained beside Marek, shoulders squared, faces grim.

Marek didn't try to call them back. Instead, he looked to the men who stayed. "Then it's just us. See to your gear. We have work to do."

From the walls of the Ironjaw, Anya stood wrapped in her cloak, arms folded across her chest. Her eyes followed the lancers as they filed out, the morning sun glinting coldly off their armour. The sound of hooves and boots faded into the mist, a jagged reminder of how thin her cause had grown.

Her hand tightened around the hilt of her rapier, though she forced herself still. She had expected their loyalty to be tested, but watching it splinter, watching comrades tear one another apart, struck harder than she had been prepared for. More than two dozen were gone. Only four stood firm.

The northern gate closed with a heavy clang that reverberated against the walls, a stark finality to their departure.

She turned slightly to Valdek, who stood a few steps behind her. His expression was grim but steady, his eyes locking with hers. No words passed between them. Both of them knew what had been lost, and what still lay ahead.

Anya's mind shifted from disappointment to strategy. The rebellion was smaller now, the coming siege more perilous, but the Ironjaw would not fall while she drew breath.

She gripped the edge of the map spread across the battlements, her knuckles whitening as the parchment creased under her hand. Beyond the walls, the wind carried the first flakes of snow down into the valley, a quiet herald of the long, hard trial to come.

She whispered under her breath, almost to herself, "We will hold, we must."

Chapter Twelve

One month had passed since the lancers' departure, and the Ironjaw had transformed from a simple guardhouse into a fortress bristling with defences. Trenches had been dug along the approaches, barricades reinforced, and makeshift palisades erected where the stone walls were weak. The rebels had drilled relentlessly, the clang of hammer on anvil echoing from the forge as Daran and his team repaired weapons and armour for every able fighter.

The Shatter Tooth scouts returned from the northern ridges, faces grim beneath the hoods of their furs. They huddled with Anya and her captains in the command tent, reporting what they had seen.

"Protectorate forces are on the march," one scout said, voice low. "A large column, nearly two thousand strong. Cavalry in the vanguard. They are pushing hard through the southern valleys, likely to reach Ironjaw in two days' time."

Valdek frowned, rubbing the back of his neck. "They're moving faster than we anticipated. They must have intelligence about our position."

Banu's hand rested on the hilt of his curved blade. "We've done all we could to mask our movements. Haldic must have told them."

Anya's eyes narrowed, her jaw set. "It doesn't matter how they know. We prepare. We hold the walls. Nothing gets through our gates without paying a price."

Tareq stepped forward, glancing at the gathered rebels. "We don't have the numbers, but they will expect us to defend the walls directly. We can use the terrain, traps, and every advantage we've got."

The scouts nodded. "The river to the east can be diverted, the cliffs can be used to funnel them. But they are coming fast."

Anya's gaze swept over the assembled captains. "Then we make every moment count. Every wall, every spike, every soldier will matter. We've trained for this. We fight together. And we will not fall."

A tense silence settled over the room. Outside, the wind carried the faint clatter of preparations. The sharpening of blades, the hauling of stones, the murmured words of warriors bracing for the storm that would soon descend upon the Ironjaw.

***

The morning air was crisp, carrying the distant sound of hooves and the noise of men assembling for war. Down the valley, the Protectorate force stretched in a seemingly endless line, banners snapping in the wind, armour glinting in the sun. Cavalry circled the flanks while infantry moved in tight formation toward the Ironjaw.

From the walls, the defenders strained their eyes. Archers scrambled to the battlements, quivers full, bows at the ready. Siege engines were readied, boiling oil hauled into position, and rebels took their stations along the ramparts. Every hand counted, every heartbeat measured against the growing threat.

Then, a lone rider broke from the main formation. Heavy plate catching the sunlight, a pale blue plume atop his helm swaying as he rode forward. The line of the army seemed to part unconsciously for him, allowing his slow, deliberate approach.

The rider brought his mount to a halt just outside the effective range of the archers on the wall. With a careful movement, he dismounted, the heavy metal sections of his armour clanked together with every step. His boots crunched against the stones, and he walked toward the walls with a steady, measured pace.

On the battlements, Anya watched intently. "Don't shoot," she called. Her voice carried easily along the ramparts. "Wait and see what he intends."

The defenders hesitated, gripping their bows tighter. Even the Shatter Tooth leaned forward, keen eyes tracking each step of the lone figure. Every instinct told them to be ready for battle, yet the rider's calm, deliberate gait gave the impression he was not here to charge.

He stopped a few dozen paces from the base of the walls, raising one gauntleted hand as if to speak, and the valley fell into an uneasy hush. The tension was palpable, the air thick with the scent of sweat, leather, and the faint tang of fear.

Anya took a slow breath, resting one hand lightly on the hilt of her rapier. Her mind raced with possibilities. Was this a challenge? A messenger? Or a trap set by the magisters?

The rider's shadow stretched long across the stone, and all eyes followed his deliberate motions, waiting for the first words to shatter the silence that now fell on the Ironjaw.

***

The rider's voice boomed across the valley, carrying easily to the top of the walls of the Ironjaw. "False Tsarevna Anya Velmira! You will descend and meet with me. You may bring any number of guards you desire."

The battlements fell silent. Arrows rested on bowstrings, eyes squinting against the sun, every rebel holding their breath.

Valdek stepped beside Anya, his expression grave. "This is madness! You cannot go, it is a trap. They will have prepared every trick to take you, to stop the fight before it even begins."

Anya's jaw set, her eyes narrowing as she studied the rider. The shine of polished armour, the deliberate calm in his stance, the sheer audacity of calling her out. It was exactly the type of challenge she could not ignore.

"I have to go," she said, her voice firm. "If I refuse, it will be taken as a sign of weakness. They will exploit it and continue striking at the fort while I hesitate. I will not allow others to die in my place."

Tareq and Daran exchanged a glance, a silent understanding passing between them. Tareq's hand brushed the edge of his mask, his other fingers flexing in anticipation of combat. "We're going with you," he said. "If it's a trap, we won't let them take you."

Daran's prosthetic fingers flexed, his other hand gripping tightly around the head of his hammer. He nodded once, his dark eyes hard. "We face this together."

Anya allowed herself a brief, faint smile. "Then let's go."

With that, she descended from the battlements, her rapier and dagger at her side, Tareq and Daran following closely behind her. The rebel forces on the walls watched silently. Tension tightening every shoulder, every grip on sword and bow. None of them moved to interfere.

The Ironjaw's gates loomed behind them, the narrow valley stretching out to the lone rider waiting below. The wind carried the scent of stone and pine, and in that moment, every heartbeat seemed to echo like a drumbeat heralding the coming storm.

The three of them stepped out into the open, approaching the rider whose challenge had drawn them from the safety of their walls.

As they drew closer, Tareq's eyes caught a glint on the polished steel of the rider's breastplate. He squinted and then cursed under his breath. "Look at that," he muttered to Anya and Daran. "VII. He is from the Blackhold, another one of their experiments."

Daran's gaze sharpened, scanning the knight's stance and movements. Everything about him felt wrong, almost too controlled, too deliberate. "An essence user…" he said quietly. "Like us."

They slowed as they reached speaking distance. Anya stepped forward, rapier and dagger at her side but held loosely, with a commanding presence radiating from her. "State your purpose," she said. Her voice carried authority, even across the open ground.

The knight raised his visor slightly, revealing a pale, scarred face beneath. His tone was cold, every word precise. "Tsarevna Anya Velmira," he said, his voice echoing slightly through the valley, "you and your forces are ordered to surrender immediately to the Protectorate of Magisters. Any resistance will be met with total annihilation."

He took a deliberate step closer, lowering his visor fully and addressing her with an unusual familiarity. "Malyshka," he said, the word somehow stuck with quiet affection, "do you truly believe you can defy the Protectorate?"

As the knight lowered his visor, Anya felt a flicker of something deep in her chest. She froze. The sting of a name she had not heard in many years stirred something long buried.

Her hand tightened around the rapier. "How do you know that name?" she demanded, her voice sharp, demanding, but laced with fear.

The knight did not answer immediately. He simply shifted, the sun glinting off the polished engravings of VII on his breastplate, the metallic shifting of his movements echoing faintly. His tone remained cold, precise. "It was a name used by only one person. Isn't that right, malyshka?"

Tareq noticed the slight pause in her stance and frowned. "Anya?" he asked cautiously. "What is it?"

She blinked rapidly, fighting the swirl of memories the word had stirred. Faces from the past, voices long-forgotten, lessons whispered in secrecy. They all rushed back her now, in fragments. "It… it's a name from my past," she admitted, voice tight. "One I hoped never to hear again."

Daran's eyes narrowed, sensing the shift in her focus. "We don't have time," he said, his tone firm. "Whoever he is, he's here to fight."

The knight drew his weapons with mechanical precision. From his saddle came a worn mace, dented from countless battles, and in his other hand, a side sword gleamed in the morning sun. Every movement spoke of years of training, of a lifetime shaped by war and service. Anya's chest tightened as she looked at him, the pieces finally snapping into place.

Her eyes narrowed. There was no doubt now.

"Branislav!" she called, her voice cutting across the valley, firm and commanding. "You don't need to do this! For any love or loyalty you once held for my family, for any honour you still remember, stand with us now!"

The knight's eyes flickered with the faintest trace of regret hidden behind a mask of duty. He lowered his sword slightly, but his mace remained ready.

"I am sorry, malyshka," he said, his voice low and solemn. Every word carried the weight of years of conflict and impossible choices. "This is the only chance for you to avoid suffering. It is all I can do."

Anya felt a stab of pain at his words. The loss of trust mingled with the fire of determination inside her. Her grip tightened on her rapier. "There is still time to do the right thing, Branislav," she said, her voice unwavering. "Join us now, or this ends here."

He glanced past her, over the gathered rebellion, over the banners fluttering in the wind, and over the faces of those who had suffered under the magisters' hands. His expression softened for a heartbeat before the weight of duty returned. "I... I cannot defy them, no one can resist them."

The tension between them was palpable, a fragile thread holding the moment together. Every soldier, every bowman, every watchful eye on the walls seemed to hold its breath. The bridge between loyalty, duty, and old bonds was narrower than ever.

***

Branislav's feet pounded against the earth as he charged, his mace swinging in a wide arc.

Tareq moved swiftly to stand in front of Anya, his twin curved swords raised. The first strike from Branislav came at a high diagonal, aimed to take Tareq's head off. He twisted, parrying wildly with the flat of one blade while the other slashed to deflect the short sword. Sparks flew as steel clashed against steel, and the sound echoed through the valley.

Branislav did not pause. The mace came down hard, smashing against Tareq's crossed blades. The force rattled his arms and pushed him back several steps, but he recovered quickly, rolling aside to avoid the follow-up swing. Each strike Branislav made was calculated, testing reactions, looking for a chance to break through his defence.

Anya kept her rapier poised, moving as close as she could to flank him, but she did not dare fully commit. Her eyes tracked every motion, searching for an opening, ready to exploit any mistake. Tareq's body was a shield, his swords dancing in arcs of fire and steel, keeping the fallen knight at bay while Anya prepared herself for the decisive moment.

Branislav's eyes flicked briefly toward Anya, a mixture of regret and focus, before snapping back to Tareq. He feinted with a thrust from his sword, then brought the mace down in a crushing blow, forcing Tareq to twist violently, letting the strike slam into the dirt beneath them with a resounding crack. Dust and grit flew into the air, stinging their eyes.

Tareq forced a grin, parrying once again, sweat and blood mingling on his brow, running down the seam between flesh and metal. Tareq's twin curved swords spun in arcs, fighting violently for every step, his voice carrying over the clash of steel. "Anytime you're ready!" he shouted, glancing briefly at Daran and Anya.

Daran stepped forward, hefting his hammer in one hand and a chunk of stone in the other, eyes fixed on Branislav. With a roar, he swung the stone, smashing it against the ground just beside the knight's feet. The impact sent shards of stone flying and forced Branislav to step back, breaking his rhythm for a heartbeat.

Anya mirrored Daran's move, her rapier flashing as she moved to flank Branislav from the opposite side. She didn't attack yet, still maintaining measure. Her eyes tracked every twitch, every shift of weight in the knight's stance, knowing he was biding his time, waiting for them to make a single mistake, just as they were.

Branislav's eyes flicked between the three of them, realizing he could no longer face Tareq alone. His sword swung to intercept Daran's approach while his mace whipped toward Tareq in a deadly arc. Sparks flew from metal on metal and stone against steel, each strike echoing over the walls and down the valley.

Tareq grinned, adrenaline sharpening his senses. "Now!" he yelled. The three moved as one, an unstoppable force converging on Branislav.

A sudden blast of wind tore across the valley floor, slamming Daran, Tareq, and Anya back several paces. Dust and debris swirled around them, forcing them to brace themselves. Branislav's voice cut through the chaos, calm yet edged with menace. "I could end this quickly. I could pull the air from your lungs, Malyshka. But you deserve better than that."

Anya's grip tightened on her rapier, her eyes narrowing as she studied him. Sparks danced along the edge of his sword, the swirling air wrapping around it like living tendrils. Tiny arcs of lightning sparked from the metal, illuminating his pale eyes beneath the visor.

Tareq moved closer, one sword raised high, the other low, flames licking faintly along their edges, pulled from the burner at his waist. "We've survived worse than this," he shouted, keeping his footing against the gusts of wind.

Daran steadied himself, drawing stone and dirt from the ground towards his prosthetic arm, forming a shield, placing himself slightly ahead of Anya. "Don't underestimate us," he growled, feeling the raw elemental power radiating from Branislav's blade. With a controlled motion, he slammed his hammer against the stone beneath him, sending a small spray of rubble toward the knight as a distraction.

Branislav's eyes gleamed with cold calculation. He swung the sword in a wide arc, the charged air slicing through the space in front of him. The lightning crackled along the metal, and the wind whipped like a living thing. Anya pivoted just in time, her rapier slicing the air to redirect some of the blast, while Tareq spun his blades in a protective circle, flames flaring outward.

The air hummed with energy as Branislav advanced, each step stirred gusts that threatened to knock the rebels off balance. Lightning arced unpredictably, striking the cobblestones and sending shards flying. Daran planted his feet firmly, raising his shield. With a low grunt, he slammed it into the ground, sending another ripple of stone upward, disrupting the currents of wind aimed at them.

Tareq leapt forward, flames coiling around his twin curved swords like living serpents. He darted between the blasts, slashing toward Branislav's legs to force him backward, his fire illuminating the stormy valley in bursts of orange and gold. Sparks collided with arcs of lightning, hissing as energy met energy.

Anya spun gracefully, rapier flashing in her hands. Each thrust and parry cut through wind and debris, her movements precise and fluid. She targeted openings in Branislav's defence, her blade a needle, weaving against the gusts and the crackling sword. With each strike, she forced him to adjust, to split his attention between three opponents instead of two.

Branislav roared in frustration, swinging his mace with brutal force, each heavy blow sending tremors across the ground. Daran caught the impact on his hammer, letting it absorb the shock while simultaneously using the momentum to smash a jagged chunk of stone toward Branislav. The piece of rubble struck him in the side, sending a jolt through his body and disrupting the currents around him.

Tareq saw the opening and called out, the flames flaring higher along his blades. He spun in a wide arc, unleashing a wave of fire that forced Branislav to retreat a step, giving Anya just enough space to thrust her rapier into the gap at his guard. The lightning sputtered as it met the rapier's steel, arcs fizzing harmlessly into the air.

Daran's voice boomed, carrying over the storm. "Now, Tareq! Now, Anya!"

Working in perfect harmony, the three rebels pressed the attack. Tareq's fire forced Branislav backward, Daran's hammer shattered the stones beneath him, making him lose his footing, and Anya's rapier probed for weakness. Each move was calculated, each strike coordinated, a symphony of elemental and physical power.

Branislav stumbled, fury radiating through his heavy armour. The wind that had been his shield now became a liability, buffeting him unpredictably. Sparks flew along his sword, lightning snapping erratically as he tried to maintain control.

The rebels were relentless. Their bond was forged in months of survival and shared hardship. Together, they pushed Branislav to the very edge of the valley, the storm of fire, stone, and steel overwhelming his defences.

Branislav's swings became more erratic, lightning and wind crackling around him as he searched for an opening. Tareq's flames licked at his sides, forcing him to dodge rather than strike, while Daran's hammer shattered more of the ground underfoot, each slam sending tremors through the uneven stones.

Anya moved with careful precision. Her eyes locked on the narrow eye slit of Branislav's helm. In her left hand, the sapphire-pommelled dagger glinted, ready to end this.

Suddenly, Branislav lashed out with a brutal, unexpected cut aimed directly at Anya. She saw it too late. From her current position, extended in a thrust, her reflexes alone would not be enough to save her.

Daran reacted instantly and thrust his shielded arm into the path of the blade. The sword tore through the reinforced limb, severing it cleanly near the elbow. Sparks of pain and shock rippled through him, but he did not falter.

Anya froze for a heartbeat, heart hammering, and then surged forward. With a final, fluid motion, she lunged, guiding the dagger through the eye slit of Branislav's helmet. The sapphire in the pommel caught the light as it pierced deep, and Branislav's howl of disbelief and pain cut through the windstorm he had created.

Branislav crumpled to the ground, his lightning-tinged wind dissipating into the sky. The metallic hum of his sword faded, leaving only the distant clatter of the Protectorate forces waiting further down the valley. Anya pulled her dagger free, her arms trembling from the effort and adrenaline, but her gaze never wavered from the fallen knight.

Daran stumbled backward, gripping the stump of his left. Pain radiated

sharply up his arm, but his jaw tightened against it. He had faced worse, and he

knew the fight was far from over. Tareq dropped to one knee beside him,

flames flickering faintly around his hands, shielding Daran from any stray

elemental backlash.

"Stay with me," Tareq said, voice low but urgent.

Anya nodded, panting, then turned her attention to the ornate dagger, the one

that he had given her, now smeared with a mix of blood and dirt. She wiped

the blade against her leg, then locked eyes with Branislav. "It ends here," she

said, her voice steady despite the storm of emotions inside her.

Tareq placed a hand on Daran's shoulder. "You're still standing. That counts

for everything."

Above them, the sun broke through the clouds, scattering light across the

battlefield. The storm of elemental power that had surrounded Branislav

moments ago was gone.

Anya sheathed her dagger and moved closer to Daran. "We've bought the

others time. Now we need to regroup and prepare for what comes next."

Tareq's flames died down, leaving only warmth, and he nodded. "Agreed.

But first, we need to make sure he cannot rise again."

Anya's gaze lingered on Branislav one last time. Even in death, his presence seemed to haunt the empty courtyard. Victory felt hollow; beyond the walls, the enemy army still stood, vast and unyielding, a reminder that this battle was only a single step in a far longer fight.

She turned back toward the Ironjaw gate, determination hardening her features, ready to face the weeks to come.

***

The siege stretched into its second month, the days blurring together in a haze of cold wind, smoke from the cooking fires, and the muffled thud of siege engines against the Ironjaw's outer walls.

From the ramparts, Anya watched the enemy camp shift and change. New tents rose. Old ones were burned or moved. The magisters' forces were patient, almost unnervingly so, their banners snapping in the wind like a warning. They had yet to commit to a full assault again, and that, more than anything, gnawed at the defenders' nerves. Something was coming.

Within the fortress, Daran's recovery became a small beacon of resilience. His work on a new prosthesis turned into a spectacle for the troops.

One afternoon, the forge roared to life, filling the air with heat, smoke, and the tang of molten metal. Daran sat on a low bench with the beginnings of the new arm spread across the table. His whole body twitched involuntarily as phantom pain shot through his missing arm. A sharp twinge made him flinch, and he clenched his jaw against the wave of nausea that followed.

"Steady," he muttered to himself, flexing the stump. Sweat stung his eyes. Every change, every screw tightened, sent echoes of old pain up his arm. His body screamed for rest, for rest, but he ignored it. With careful precision, he began assembling the heavy plates along the forearm. Each joint, each hinge, was a battle against his own nerves.

Sparks flew as he tested the first movement. A shudder ran through him. Metal and stone fingers curled and pulled as if the arm remembered the strike it would deliver. He gritted his teeth and pushed on, tightening a final screw. The steel digits flexed and curled with a quiet click.

Hours passed. The forge's roar became a drumbeat, punctuated by the hiss of molten metal and the clang of hammers. Soldiers, bandits, and even Shatter Tooth warriors lingered at the edge of his forge, watching the sparks fly. The design differed from his old one. This arm had heavy plates along the forearm, stronger joints in the fingers, and a built-in catch for holding an earthen shield more securely. It was more than a replacement limb. Now it was a weapon.

"You're making it dangerous," Tareq remarked one afternoon, leaning in the doorway with arms crossed.

"That's the point," Daran replied without looking up, flexing the steel digits again. "Last time, it was just a magister experiment. This time... it's more."

***

Food was still coming in through secret routes through the mountains, but less each week. Water was rationed. The wounded outnumbered the fresh. They took turns sleeping in their armour, afraid of a sudden night attack. The rest of the Flying Stags, restless by nature, clashed more often with the other fortress guards. Valdek had to break up a fight between them and a Shatter Tooth tribesman over nothing more than a half-empty barrel of apples.

Anya still kept the council steady, making her presence known on the walls and in the mess halls, even when exhaustion hollowed her eyes. She couldn't let the defenders see her falter.

Then, on the thirty-ninth day, the enemy changed their rhythm.

At dawn, the usual scattered calls of morning from the magister camp were replaced by silence. From the walls, the defenders watched as a new detachment arrived. Armoured in blackened steel, carrying siege towers painted with the Protectorate's crest. These were not the rabble or mercenary auxiliaries who had been harrying the fortress. This was the elite magister guard, and they had come for the kill.

The Ironjaw would not hold forever, and everyone within the walls knew it.

***

The council chamber was colder than usual, the torches along the walls burning low as if even the fire felt the weight of what was coming. Maps of the surrounding terrain lay spread across the table, marked with hurried charcoal lines and circles where scouts had reported enemy movements.

Anya stood at the head, her palms flat against the scarred wood. "They'll be ready to assault in force within the day," she said, voice steady despite the knot in her chest. "The Ironjaw will fall. If we're to preserve what remains of the rebellion, we must get our people out before that happens."

Marek's jaw tightened. "Through the pass? In daylight? They'll be cut down."

"Not if someone buys them time," Tareq said from his place near the door. He stepped forward, leaning casually on the table, though he had difficulty reading the map with his one good eye. "A small force could hold the enemy outside the gate long enough for the rest to slip away. Most of their numbers are in the siege towers, so they won't be able to pivot them."

Daran, seated with his new prosthesis resting heavily on the arm of the chair, didn't hesitate. "I'll go with you."

Anya's gaze snapped to him. "No. You're still recovering."

"I'm recovered enough," he said flatly, flexing the metal fingers. The movement was slow but deliberate, the faint click of the joints echoing in the silence. "This is what I built this for. And you'll need both of us if you want enough time."

Tareq gave a small, humourless smile. "Besides, who else is going to stop me from doing something stupid?"

A murmur passed through the gathered leaders. Banu scowled but didn't argue. Valdek shook his head. Marek avoided Anya's eyes, his knuckles white from gripping the edge of the table.

Marek's voice rose, sharp with frustration. "Tsarevna, you can't let them do this. You will get yourselves killed for nothing! This isn't just your fight."

Anya's hands curled into fists. "If you do this, you may not make it out."

Tareq shrugged. "Then make sure that the rest do. That's the point, isn't it?"

Daran's voice was quieter, but heavier. "We've lost enough from running and hiding. Let's win something, just this once."

The silence that followed was broken only by the low crackle of the torches. Finally, Anya nodded, though it felt like swallowing broken glass. "Then we make every moment count, but...."

The weight in the room seemed to shift as Anya straightened, her eyes moving from Tareq to Daran, then to the others gathered around the table.

"You will not do this alone," she said.

Tareq frowned. "Anya…"

"I have made my choice," she cut him off. "If this is to be our last stand, then I will be there with you. Valdek will take command of the rebellion."

Valdek's head jerked up, eyes wide. "Tsarevna, no!"

"Yes," she said, her tone like iron. "You have commanded before, and you have fought for this cause as hard as anyone here. You are as much a Velmira as I am, even if not by blood. The people will follow you."

He stared at her for a long moment, jaw tightening, then finally gave a curt nod, though his eyes were shadowed with grief. "If this is your command, I will see them to safety."

Tareq's mouth flattened into a hard line. "You are not making this easy."

"It was never meant to be easy," she replied.

The council chamber fell silent. Outside, the wind moaned through the high pass of the Ironjaw. In the quiet, the choice they had all been avoiding finally solidified. The rebellion's survival would depend on those who stayed behind, as much as those who survived.

One by one, the captains filed out, each man and woman with their own internal battles.

When the chamber was nearly empty, Daran adjusted the leather straps that kept his new prosthesis secure. "If this is it," he said quietly, "we had better make it count."

"It will count," Anya replied, her gaze lingering on the map, already plotting every moment of the fight to come.

***

That night, the fortress felt different. The usual noise of the garrison was hushed, as though every soldier was speaking in a low voice out of respect for what was to come. The moon was a pale smear through the clouds, casting faint light over the courtyards where the last supplies were packed for those who would leave before dawn.

Anya stood on the battlements for a long time, watching the glow of distant campfires from the magister army. She could almost imagine the sound of their voices drifting up the valley.

Tareq joined her, arms folded against the cold. "If you're still hoping for a miracle, you're in the wrong keep," he said.

"I stopped hoping for miracles a long time ago," she answered.

The wind bit at them on the battlements. Anya turned from the distant fires, her eyes settling on Tareq.

"Come to my room tonight," she said.

He blinked, his brow furrowing. "No, Anya."

"I want to be with someone I can trust," she continued, her voice low but steady. "Someone who will stand and fight until the end. Not like Haldic."

Tareq's gaze shifted away, the lines around his eyes deepening. "You don't know what you are asking. My face is burned. I'm a commoner. I'm a farmer's son turned bandit, and you are…"

"I am a woman who may be dead tomorrow," she interrupted. "And tonight, I don't want to be alone."

He opened his mouth to protest again, but the way she held his gaze stilled the words on his tongue. She stepped closer, her breath visible in the frigid air between them.

"Don't hide behind birth or scars, Tareq. You are more than either of those things. You have been at my side through every hardship, and I would have it no other way now."

For a moment, the only sound was the wind rushing along the stone. His jaw tightened, then loosened, and something unspoken passed between them.

Later, as they lay together, Anya's fingers traced the burned lines on his face, each scar a reminder of everything they had lost, and everything they might never see again. Tareq lay there quietly, staring at the ceiling, the timbers of the fortress groaning under the wind like the battlefield itself. Every whisper of air through the walls carried the weight of the coming siege. This was their last

night of quiet. Tomorrow, fire and blood would claim the fortress, and

whatever peace they had found in each other tonight.

Chapter Thirteen

Anya awoke to a low, undulating chant that seemed to roll across the camp like a living thing. Beneath it, drums pounded in a steady, hypnotic rhythm. Each strike resonating through the cold stone walls and into her chest, as if calling to something unseen. She swung her legs over the edge of her cot, heart quickening, and moved toward the source of the sound.

The air outside was sharp with frost, but thick smoke and the acrid scent of burning herbs curled around her, carrying a metallic tang that made her stomach turn. In the courtyard, the Shatter Tooth had gathered, forming a living spiral around a bonfire that burned brighter than any ordinary flame. It flickered with colours that did not belong to fire of the natural world. Green and violet tongues licked at the air, casting twisted shadows that danced along the walls of the Ironjaw.

The warriors moved in unison. Their chants rising and falling in impossible harmonies. Some swung their curved knives, others clutched bones strung with feathers, striking the ground in time with the drums, which now seemed to vibrate with a resonance that made the hairs on Anya's arms stand on end.

At the centre by the fire, Ula held a goat, its eyes wide with panic, yet its body seemed to shimmer in the firelight, like it existed on two worlds at once. She raised her curved blade, and when it struck, a thin ribbon of flame leapt from the wound, twisting upward before vanishing into smoke. The sound from the sacrifice was muffled, as though swallowed by the chant, and a faint hum filled the courtyard.

Anya's voice trembled. "What... what is this?"

Ula's pale eyes locked on hers, unblinking, calm. "This is a sacrifice," she said, voice low but carrying an eerie weight. "We honour our mistress, calling her favour. So that you three may carry her blessing into the fight to come."

Anya watched, transfixed, as the Shatter Tooth continued their dance. The flames twisted unnaturally, shadows moving independently of the dancers. The air thrummed with a strange energy, and Anya felt a prickling along her skin, as if the ritual itself was watching and measuring the worth of those who would call for aid.

For a moment, the chaos of war, the fear and stakes of the fight ahead crystallised in the fire and smoke and the brutality of the ceremony. She could feel the faint pulse of something larger, something both ancient and patient, threading through the chant and the flames, tethering her to her companions.

***

As the sun rose, they stood in the courtyard, their armour buckled and weapons in hand. The air was still sharp with the smell of the ritual fire. Above them, Sokol circled high, his cry carrying across the walls, sharper and more urgent than usual.

Tareq tilted his head back to watch the bird. "Even he knows something's coming," he muttered.

He shifted his gaze to the others, a faint spark in his eyes despite the weight of what lay ahead. "We need something special to be remembered by," he said, almost as if he were trying to pull them all into the same reckless thought.

Anya raised an eyebrow at him. "Special?"

"Something they'll still talk about when our bones are dust," Tareq replied, with a wide grin that was still visible under his mask.

He scanned the courtyard, eyes darting over the battered walls and frost-bitten barrels before coming to rest on a freshly butchered deer hanging from a hook, it's blood still dripping in slowly into the dirt. The smell of raw meat was thick in the air. His gaze slid past it toward a heap of discarded saddle banners from one of the eastern lancers, their bold colours dulled by grime.

A slow, wolfish grin spread further across his face.

"Oh no," Daran muttered, bracing himself.

Tareq turned to him, grin widening. "Oh yes. If we're going to make a last stand, we might as well look like something out of the old songs."

Anya crossed her arms. "And what exactly are you thinking?"

Daran snorted. "You want to go into battle dressed like a madman."

"I want to leave this battle remembered," Tareq said simply. "If today is the day I die, it's better I go looking like the gods themselves spat me back into this world."

For a moment, Anya just stared at him, then a small, dangerous smile tugged at her lips. "Fine. Let's make them believe the old legends are true."

***

The portcullis of the northern gate groaned open, the heavy chains rattling like the final toll of a bell. Cold air swept through the Ironjaw courtyard, carrying the faint scent of smoke and iron. Beyond the gate, the field stretched toward the horizon, dark with the silhouettes of the Protectorate's forces. In the distance, war drums thundered and horns blared, their echoes bouncing across the mountains.

Anya moved first, her rapier catching the sun, shards of light scattering across the stones. Her body was coiled for the strike, every step controlled.

Tareq and Daran fell in behind her. A silent, deadly trio crossed the threshold from safety into the storm.

Tareq was almost unrecognizable. The torn banners of the eastern lancers lashed to his back, snapping in the wind, and the skull of the butchered deer crowning his head, its sockets stared hollowly and unblinking. Each step he took made the skull tilt slightly, lending him a monstrous, otherworldly presence.

Daran's brow furrowed as he looked at his companion. "You still look like an idiot," he muttered, a dry note of disbelief in his voice.

Tareq turned his head slightly, a grin visible beneath the bone mask. "Just wait," he said. His voice carried a quiet confidence that made Daran's words fade, as if he already knew the outcome of the next few moments. There was something in that grin, a promise that the Protectorate would remember the sight, if not the man himself.

The gate slammed shut behind them, reverberating off the valley's walls. The Ironjaw Gates, their bastion for so long, was now behind them. Retreat was no longer an option. They moved forward with the wind at their backs, the banners flapping and the deer skull glistening in the light, a grim herald of what was to come. Every step brought them closer to the enemy, closer to the point of no return.

Even as the first shouts of the Protectorate reached their ears, even as the

their arms and armour reflected in the morning sun, there was an undeniable

sense of destiny. Tareq's eccentric display was not merely decoration. They

were not just charging into battle, they were making a mark on Rosk that

would not soon be forgotten.

***

The narrow mountain pass echoed with the clatter of armour and the

rhythmic pounding of hundreds of marching feet. Dust rose in clouds around

the advancing Protectorate forces, their spears and banners shining in the pale

sunlight. Tareq stepped forward from the line, the small iron lantern at his hip

swinging slightly.

He called to the fire within, and the flames leapt eagerly, licking up the

curved blades of his twin swords. The winged banners strapped to his back

ignited, their tattered fabric hissing and curling as the fire transformed them

into burning wings. The antlers of the deer skull atop his head caught the blaze

as well, casting flickering shadows across his face. With each movement, he

seemed less human, more a creature of legend. He seemed like the fallen gods

of old, risen to cast judgment.

He raised one sword high, with the fire trailing behind it, and shouted across

the pass. His voice rang with authority and fury, cutting through the sound of the approaching army. "I am Tareq, son of Jahlan Sword-Hand, chieftain of the Flying Stags! You will not leave here alive!"

The flames danced along his figure, twisting around him like a living aura, and for a moment the soldiers in the Protectorate ranks faltered. Their confidence wavered as they took in the sight, a single warrior, monstrous and radiant in fire, daring them to advance.

Tareq let out a fierce cry and swung his flaming sword in a wide arc, sparks spraying outward, and the heat of the flames carried forward, singeing the edges of the first rows of advancing troops. The mountain pass, once a simple route of trade, had transformed into a crucible of fire and vengeance. Every eye was on him. Every heart felt the weight of the challenge he posed.

He stood tall, a figure of terror and defiance, daring the Protectorate army to come closer, daring them to test the wrath of a son of the Flying Stags, and the heart of the rebellion.

***

The trio surged forward. The canyon walls narrowed, funnelling the clash. Dust and smoke mingled with the heat of Tareq's flaming swords and banners, the flickering firelight painting the rocky walls in an otherworldly glow.

With each step, the ground trembled beneath Daran. Stones tore free, orbiting him before fusing into a towering husk of earth. His voice rumbled, heavier now, like bedrock grinding.

"Come closer."

The golem he had once proclaimed to the magi he could not become now stood before them, a living embodiment of his wrath and fury.

Tareq led the charge, the heat from his swords and banners casting waves of shimmering light across the ranks of the advancing army. Behind him, Anya ran with her rapier and dagger gleaming, her eyes cold and determined, moving with precision, ready to strike at any opening.

The first wave of Protectorate riders met them, and Daran swung his colossal, barrel-like fist. The impact was absolute. A horse and its rider vanished under the blow, rock and debris scattering in every direction. The mountain itself seemed alive with their fury, the force of the strike sending shockwaves up the mountain pass.

Tareq spun, the flames along his curved swords tracing arcs of fire, slashing through spears and shields, while Anya darted to the side, her rapier stabbing and cutting with deadly efficiency. The ground trembled beneath Daran's feet, forcing the enemy lines to break, panic spreading as the sheer size and power of the stone golem collided with disciplined formations.

The battlefield had become an inferno of fire, stone, and steel. Every step Daran took was a declaration, every swing of Tareq's flaming blades a warning, and every strike of Anya's rapier a promise that they would not be stopped. The rebellion would not be stopped.

The Protectorate forces faltered, their cohesion breaking under the combined might of the three, as the rebellion's champions drove them backward, step by step, down the pass. The roar of the mountain, the clash of metal, and the crackling of fire filled the air, the legend of crown, fire and stone being forged with every step.

***

High above, Sokol circled in tight, screaming loops, his piercing cries carrying across the canyon. The sharp, commanding sound of horns echoed from the Protectorate lines below, a signal for retreat, while farther off, from the eastern ridge, a second set of horns blared in urgent rhythm, calling for a charge.

Tareq skidded to a halt, the flaming banners and antlered skull casting wild shadows on the jagged rocks beneath their feet. He glanced at Daran with confusion written across his soot-streaked face.

"What is going on?" Tareq shouted, his voice barely audible over the din.

Daran's massive stone-encased form trembled slightly as he came to a stop, fists raised, surveying the battlefield. He could feel the tension in the air, the way the vibrations of the horns carried differently across the mountain slopes. His stone-clad voice boomed like shifting earth. "Two signals... not one command. Something else moves."

Anya, still gripping her rapier tightly, scanned the horizon with sharp, calculating eyes. Her stance was steady, but her brow furrowed. "One group retreats. The other charges…"

Sokol screeched again, diving low and then climbing high, his wings casting shadows like a living banner over the battlefield. The falcon's movements seemed frantic, urging them to pay attention, yet revealing nothing clearly.

Tareq shook his head, flames flickering across his swords. "I don't like this."

Daran's massive stone form shifted, the earth around him groaning under his weight. "We hold," he said finally. "We wait and see. One wrong step and the Protectorate will exploit it."

Anya nodded, eyes narrowing, the wind tugging at her cloak. "Then we wait. And when the moment comes, we strike with everything we have."

The three of them stood side by side, the ground beneath trembled with Daran's presence, Tareq's flames danced, and Anya's rapier glinted in the harsh morning light, the tension thick and electric as the conflicting sounds of horns echoed across the mountains.

***

Then, from the canyon below, banners of deep blue unfurled. A thunder of hooves shook the ground as a large regiment of cavalry surged forward through the magister's ranks. Winged banners streamed behind each horse like great living wings, catching the sunlight and dazzling the eye. Screams and the clash of steel filled the air as the enemy lines faltered. Magister infantry and cavalry alike scattered before the unstoppable charge, those that reacted too slowly were trampled beneath the wave of hooves.

Tareq's eye widened as he took in the spectacle, flames flickering along his swords and the antlered skull strapped to his head. "By the gods," he muttered, gripping his weapons tighter. Daran's massive stone-encased fists clenched, shaking the ground with every step as he prepared to crush any remaining resistance.

For a moment, Anya's breath caught. She knew that formation. Sokol dove low over the blue banners, screaming.

The horsemen wheeled with precision, creating a protective barrier around the trio. At the head of the charge remained the leader. Tall and commanding, his polished armour gleaming with sapphire highlights. A long cloak of deep blue swirled behind him, and a falcon insignia glinted on his chest plate.

Ksiaze Boris Sobieska dismounted smoothly, the reins of his mount slipped from his gloved hands without a second thought. He surveyed the battlefield, then fixed his calm, unwavering gaze on Anya. His voice rang clearly across the din of battle, carrying authority and warmth in equal measure. "Hello, Cousin," he said, a faint smile tugging at his lips. "I heard that some of my men disobeyed their orders and stayed to fight beside you. It is not our way to leave the fight to others."

Anya blinked, taken aback for only a moment. Recognition flared within her, a mixture of relief and surprise. Tareq let out a low whistle, muttering something about being glad he wasn't on the receiving end of that cavalry charge.

The blue banners surged forward, cutting a swath through the magisters' remaining forces. Horses collided with enemy lines, lances shattered against shields, and cries of fear and defiance echoed across the pass. With such an immense force of eastern lancers, the tide of battle started to turn. The once-impregnable Protectorate force faltered under the sudden, overwhelming assault.

Boris stepped closer to Anya, lowering his voice slightly, pulling her into a tight embrace. "You are not alone in this fight. Let's finish what you started."

Anya exhaled, feeling a weight lift from her shoulders. She straightened, gripping her rapier and looking to her friends, her voice firm and clear. "Then let us end this."

***

The thunder of hooves shook the mountain pass as Ksiaze Boris's eastern lancers surged forward, their blue winged banners snapping in the wind. Each horseman was a whirlwind of discipline and fury, cutting through the

Protectorate lines with precise, devastating strikes. The magisters' remaining forces, already shaken by the rebel trio, faltered under the sudden, coordinated onslaught.

Tareq led the way. Flames streaked around him, and with each swing of his twin blades, soldiers were thrown back or scorched where they stood. His presence alone was enough to scatter smaller units, leaving them disoriented and terrified.

Daran moved like a living fortress behind him, his massive stone-form smashed through cavalry and infantry alike. Fists the size of boulders crushed both men and mounts with brutal efficiency. Each step left craters in the ground, creating new obstacles that slowed and disorganised the magisters' formations.

Anya was a blade of precision in the chaos, her rapier flashing as she cut a path through anyone attempting to flank her friends. With every strike, she reminded the Protectorate forces why she bore the Velmira name. Her movements were swift and controlled, a deadly contrast to the raw, destructive power of Tareq and Daran.

The eastern lancers under Boris's leadership pressed in like a tidal wave. Spears and curved sabres met the enemy from every angle, while riders wheeled to protect gaps in the trio's line. Boris himself charged at the centre of the magisters' formation, cutting down elite guards with swift, disciplined strikes. His presence inspired the lancers, and they responded with unmatched coordination, routing the enemy from the flanks.

The air above the battlefield shimmered with Tareq's fire, the ground trembled beneath Daran's might, and the razor-sharp precision of Anya's rapier left no opportunity for the magisters to regroup. Soldiers who had once believed themselves invincible were thrown into confusion, many fleeing in panic, others falling to the combined assault.

From the rear, Valdek's remaining forces took advantage of the chaos. Rather than retreating as planned, he ordered them to help their Tsarevna, ambushing and capturing isolated units. Rebel banners rose across the battlefield.

As the magisters' army crumbled, the remaining commanders shouted orders in desperation, but the coordinated might of Anya, Tareq, Daran, and Boris's lancers left them with no room to manoeuvre. It was a symphony of controlled destruction, fire, earth, steel, and strategy all moving in perfect harmony.

By the time the dust settled, the magisters' forces were shattered, their banners trampled and torn. The mountain pass was littered with broken corpses and scorched earth, while victorious cries rose from the surviving rebels and lancers alike. Anya, her rapier still gleaming, looked to her friends and to Boris.

"We can do this. We will tear down their Protectorate."

The lancers roared in response, but Boris's smile was tempered, his eyes on the broken field. "Yes, cousin. But this is only the first stone toppled. The mountain still waits."

Sokol wheeled high above, his cry sharp against the silence that followed. Victory rang, yet beneath it, the wind carried the taste of battles yet to come.

Chapter Fourteen

The day after the battle, the air still smelled of smoke and blood. The cries of the wounded could be heard from the makeshift infirmary beneath the Ironjaw's shadow, where Anya moved from cot to cot, binding wounds, offering water, or simply resting a comforting hand on a shoulder. She was exhausted, her own body ached with cuts and bruises, but she would not allow herself to rest while so many others suffered.

She was kneeling beside a lancer whose leg had been shattered when Valdek emerged from the hall. His face was drawn with the weight of responsibility. He waited until Anya finished wrapping the soldier's bandages, then touched her arm gently.

"Tsarevna," he said, his voice low. "They're waiting for you."

Her brow furrowed. "Who?"

"The Ksiaze, Banu, and Ula," Valdek replied, glancing toward the great doors. "They want to speak before the magisters regroup. Yesterday's battle was a victory, but it was only the first of many to come. The Protectorate won't lick its wounds for long."

Anya exhaled slowly, her hand brushing the blood-stained cloth on her tunic. "And now they want to decide what happens next."

Valdek nodded. "The others bring banners, experience, or fear, but none of them could have held the Ironjaw as you did. They will follow, but only if you are there to guide them."

She looked once more at the wounded, at men and women who might not see another sunrise. The weight of their sacrifice pressed down on her, but their resilience stoked the fire inside her.

"Very well," she said at last. "Let them wait no longer."

Valdek offered a faint smile, though his eyes betrayed the storm of emotions he carried. Together they walked through battered corridors, the cries of the infirmary fading behind them, replaced by the steady buzz of voices ahead.

***

The great hall of the Ironjaw was dim. Its stone walls lit by the flickering glow of torches. Around the central table sat the strangest gathering Anya could have imagined. Ksiaze of the Eastern Provinces, Boris Sobieska in his blue-and-silver finery, his proud cavalry standards propped behind him. Banu al-Sayf, scarred and broad-shouldered, still wearing his blood-stained furs. Ula, pale-eyed and silent, her jagged teeth catching the light whenever her lips curled. Valdek leaned forward with the intensity of a man far younger than his years.

Tareq and Daran stood behind Anya's chair, as both her guardians and friends, as she lowered herself to the table.

Boris spoke first, voice rich and confident. "Cousin, your defence of the Ironjaw is already spreading across Rosk. The Protectorate sent its best, and you broke them. That victory must not be squandered. We must strike."

He spread his hand across the map before them, tapping the central peak that towered over the kingdom's heartlands. A jagged spire, inked in black. The High Tower.

"The seat of their power, and the ancestral home of your family. If we march swiftly, before they gather reinforcements, we can cut the head from this serpent and the body will wither. Their soldiers will lose heart without their masters to command them."

Anya studied the map in silence, her eyes narrowing. She remembered the lightning flashing from Branislav's blade, the cold familiarity in his voice when he called her malyshka. If Boris was right, there would be others like him waiting in the castle.

Banu leaned forward with a growl. "And you think your horsemen can tear down the walls of the High Tower, noble prince?" he asked with a low growl. "That fortress has stood for centuries."

Boris did not flinch. "With cavalry, militia, and Ula's... fanatics, the walls will fall. More than that, the people will rally when they see us march. An army from every corner of this land. The whole of Rosk united."

Ula finally spoke, her voice soft but edged like a knife. "The High Tower is a nest of magi. They will be waiting. They will have tricks, wards and traps. You are too eager for blood, Ksiaze Boris Sobieska, it will come in time."

Banu grunted. "For once, I agree with the cannibal."

Boris bristled, but before he could respond, Valdek's voice cut through the rising tension. "If we stay here, they will come again, but this time with greater numbers. With more knights like the one Anya defeated." He turned to her. "You saw it, Tsarevna, you know what they are building. If we wait, we give them time."

The chamber fell quiet, all eyes shifted towards Tareq and Daran.

Boris leaned forward, lowering his voice. "You have led men into fire and returned with victory. You've rallied tribes, mercenaries, lancers, outcasts. Rosk does not need a Tsarevna. It needs a Tsarina."

The words struck the room like a whip. The fire crackled, but no other movement or sound filled the room.

Banu tilted his head, a smile tugging at his lips. "Tsarina, is it? Hah. I'd ride under such a banner."

Ula's eyes gleamed in the firelight. Her teeth flashed in a predatory show. "Tsarina suits her. My people follow only strength, and I see no weakness in her."

Valdek's pointed his chin forward with pride. "Your father would have wanted this. The blood of Velmira was always meant to lead Rosk. By oath, by blood and by steel, you have proven it."

Anya sat in silence, the weight of their words pressing like iron. She remembered her father's lessons in statecraft, her mother's poise, and Branislav's cruel end. The cost of every step that brought her here. Fear twisted in her gut, though no one else could see it. They waited for her response expectantly.

Her throat felt dry as she looked to each of them. Warrior, raider, fanatic and distant family. None mocked her. Not one of them doubted her. They were waiting.

When she rose, the fire threw her shadow long. "If you insist that I be your Tsarina, I will not shrink from the duty. But hear me now, this crown will not be for thrones or glory. It is for the people who bled and died with us, and those we couldn't save. If I am Tsarina, then Rosk will never kneel to the magisters again."

The chamber stirred like a storm breaking. Boris bowed his head, satisfied. "Then it is settled. The rule of the magisters comes to an end, and the rule of House Velmira begins anew."

**

Weeks later, the rebel host marched north, swollen with lancers, tribesmen, deserters, and freedmen. Each night their campfires stretched farther across the valleys, a living river of light moving toward destiny. The land changed as they went. The rolling plains gave way to stony ridges, and then the jagged foothills of the central range.

Now they stood at the mountain's base. Above them, the High Tower pierced the sky like a pale needle of bone, half-shrouded in mist. The trail that wound its way to the summit was narrow and treacherous, a scar carved into the mountainside by centuries of travel. High above, torchlight flickered from the parapets. The magisters were watching, waiting.

The camp bustled with quiet tension. Soldiers sharpened blades by firelight, archers strung their bows, and healers prepared herbs and bandages for what was to come. This was no longer a ragged band of survivors. Under Anya's banner they had become an army. Although worn and scarred, they remained unyielding.

Tareq sat near the edge of camp, his twin blades across his knees, polishing their scorched edges with slow, deliberate strokes. His burns pulled at the skin of his face when he smiled, though his eyes betrayed no fear.

"Tomorrow, the High Tower," he muttered to himself. "Let them see what the Flying Stags have become."

Daran sat on a boulder close by, his new stone-forged arm resting heavily on his knee. He had etched words into the metal and stone, each mark a reminder of the comrades they had lost. The earth itself rumbled in his veins, restless for the fight.

Sokol circled high above the encampment, his screeches echoing against the cliffs. The falcon's presence was an omen to many of the rebels, who whispered that even the sky itself had bent to Tsarina Anya's cause.

Anya moved among the fires, her presence easing doubts. She carried her exhaustion like armour, and every gaze that met hers found strength. She was no longer only a lost daughter of Velmiran descent. She was Tsarina. Tomorrow, they would climb the winding trail. Tomorrow, the fate of Rosk would be decided.

***

In the command tent, maps and carved stones littered the table. Smoke from burning tallow curled in the air as commanders murmured.

Daran and Tareq stood together on the far side of the table, silent but steady, their loyalty to Anya unquestioned. Valdek remained close by her side, his ink-stained fingers tracing lines on the map.

Boris was the first to speak, his voice carrying the confidence and arrogance of nobility.

"The High Tower is not a simple outpost like the Ironjaw. Its defences are strong and tall. The magisters believe no army can reach them. They have not accounted for us." He leaned on the table, tapping the winding trail carved into the mountainside. "We march at dawn. My lancers can drive the vanguard up the pass. The rest of our host follows."

Banu scoffed, tossing a bone he had been gnawing on back into the firepit. "And what then, princeling? They sit on the walls with their tricks and their fire. They'll cut us to pieces on the path before we reach the gate."

"Unless," Ula hissed, her pale eyes gleaming, "we give them something else to fear. Something to make them hesitate. My people know fear is sharper than any blade." She gestured toward Anya. "You are Tsarina now. Your presence here is more than strategy, it is a weapon."

The tent grew quiet. All eyes turned to Anya.

Daran's stone arm scraped against the table as he spoke, his deep voice cutting through the silence.

"If they hold the heights, then we must tear them down. I can bring the mountain to us. Collapse their walls, drag their tower into the earth itself. But it will take time, and I'll need cover."

Tareq leaned forward then, his burned face half-lit by the lamplight. "Then that's where I come in. Let them see the Stag's wings again. Let them continue to believe the old gods of Rosk have returned to avenge their people. While they're watching me, Daran will bring the walls down."

Boris crossed his arms, frowning, but inclined his head. "Foolish or not, it has worked before. Fear wins wars."

Valdek raised his voice, calm and steady. "The magisters will not expect us to reach the gate at all. If we strike fast, they may falter before they bring their full power to bear. Our only chance is to press them, to give them no moment to recover."

The weight of the decision pressed down on the tent. Outside, the campfires crackled, and the murmurs of thousands waiting for orders drifted on the wind.

All eyes turned to Anya once more.

Anya studied the map in silence for a long moment, her hand resting near the carved stone that marked the High Tower. The others watched her, each waiting for her command.

Finally, she spoke, her voice calm, deliberate. "We cannot outmatch their sorcery, but their arrogance blinds them. Boris, keep the pass clear. Daran, bring down the gates when we are close enough to strike. Tareq, make them fear you. Ula and Banu, take the heights. Strike their flanks and divide their strength."

Banu grinned, sharp and eager, while Ula only bared her teeth in silent approval.

Daran raised his hand before speaking. "If there are so many magisters in the keep, there is something you should know. From what we saw in the Blackhold, the magisters don't need to say anything to harness essence, it's just part of their illusion."

Banu slammed his fist on the table. "You mean that all the hand waving and chanting is just for show?"

Daran nodded.

Anya straightened, her hand resting on the table.
"Thank you, Daran, but this changes nothing. When the gate falls, there will be no retreat, no pause. We press forward until the High Tower belongs to us. No mercy and no hesitation. The magisters must not rise again."

The council was silent for a breath, the weight of her words settling in. Then Boris gave a short nod of respect.
"Spoken like a true Tsarina."

One by one, the others gave their assent. The strategy was decided. At dawn, the mountain would tremble with war.

***

The camp was hushed beneath the looming shadow of the High Tower, the fires scattered among the tents burning low, their light flickering against weary faces. Somewhere in the distance, Sokol cried out before falling silent again, and the sound of restless horses carried faintly on the night air.

Tareq sat by a small fire at the edge of camp, his whetstone rasping softly against steel. Sparks danced occasionally as the blade caught the light, the rhythm steady, almost meditative. His jaw was set, eyes fixed on the edge of the sword, though his thoughts seemed elsewhere.

Daran approached quietly, his heavy steps making the earth crunch beneath him. He lowered himself to the ground beside Tareq with a slow, weary sigh. For a while, neither of them spoke. Only the scrape of steel and the crackle of the fire filled the air between them.

Finally, Tareq broke the silence. "When it's done," he said, his voice low, as if he didn't want the night to overhear, "when all of this is over... what will you do?"

Daran stared into the flames, his broad shoulders rising and falling as he considered. His stone arm rested heavily on his knee, catching the firelight like dark iron. After a long pause, he spoke. "I'll go home. Go back and rebuild my father's forge. Make it stronger than before. He always wanted me to be a master smith like he was. Perhaps it's time I finally give him that." His voice carried the weight of peace imagined, fragile and rare.

Anya slipped from the shadows, her dark hair pulled loose from its braids, her cloak wrapped tightly around her shoulders against the mountain chill. She lowered herself onto the log beside them, silent at first, listening to the tail end of their conversation.

Daran turned his pale eyes to Tareq, studying him for a moment before asking, "And you?"

The question hung in the air. The whetstone paused mid-stroke. He glanced sideways, his gaze meeting Anya's. For a moment, his hard expression softened, and then he looked back into the fire.

"I'll take the Stags," he said at last. His voice was steady, though something deeper stirred beneath it. "Back to the west. To rebuild the holds, our homes. Try to undo the destruction the magisters left behind." His grip tightened slightly on the sword hilt, knuckles whitening. "It won't be easy. But someone has to make the land live again."

The three of them sat in silence then, the fire crackling between them, each lost in their own visions of what might follow, if they survived the coming dawn.

Anya's gaze lingered on Tareq, the way his shoulders were squared as though bracing himself for burdens he hadn't yet taken on. She let the quiet stretch a little longer before speaking.

"You don't have to do it alone," Anya said softly. Both men looked at her. The firelight painted her face gold and shadow. "The west is not yours alone to bear. Rosk will need all its people made whole again. And if I am Tsarina, then no one rebuilds in isolation."

Anya drew her cloak tighter, her eyes flicking toward the distant silhouette of the High Tower. "I will build something better," she continued, voice steady despite the weight behind it, "when we beat the magisters. A court where every voice of Rosk can be heard. The northern deserts, the eastern steppes, the western plains... all of them. If Boris insists on calling me Tsarina, then I will make it mean something."

She looked back at them, firm now. "If you must go west, Tareq, you won't be abandoned to it. And if you return to your forge, Daran, the crown will not forget you either."

For a moment the fire hissed and popped, and the night seemed to fold closer around them. Tareq's grip on his blade eased, though his eyes lingered on Anya.

"You speak as though you have already won the war, and wear the crown," he murmured.

Anya's lips curved faintly, though it was not quite a smile. "Perhaps we already have."

They sat together in silence then, not with distance, but with the quiet bond of comrades who had carried too much to doubt each other now. The fire burned low, its embers glowing like the promise of dawn.

Chapter Fifteen

At first light, the rebel host began its slow climb up the winding trail toward the High Tower. The air was thin and biting, every breath laced with frost, yet no one faltered. Above, the dark spires loomed, their walls glimmering faintly with wards that caught the morning sun.

Valdek moved through the rebel camp like a cat, darting in different directions when something caught his attention. The soldiers were still gathering, adjusting armour and checking weapons.

"Listen to me!" Valdek's voice cut through the low murmur. Heads snapped toward him. "The wounded are to go to the northern tents. Splints, bandages, and pain relief are on the tables by the eastern rock face. Keep them well stocked. Nothing should be left where it can fall or be trampled."

Two healers glanced at each other, then hurried to follow his instructions. Valdek bent over a stretcher being carried by a pair of women, adjusting the blanket around a young fighter with a fractured ankle. "Extra water for the upper tents. Keep the injured away from the edges. Understand?"

By the time the drums sounded and the first soldiers began assembling to march toward the High Tower, the camp was as ready as it could be. Valdek's presence had steadied the nervous, organised the helpless, and ensured the vulnerable were shielded. He stood at the centre of the camp, shoulders squared, jaw tight, eyes tracing the winding trail above, knowing the survival of those below rested entirely on him.

***

Boris' lancers led the way, their great winged banners stretched wide, catching the wind. Their hooves struck sparks from the stones as they ascended, a wall of cavalry that seemed impossible to stop. Behind them came the infantry, grim-faced, the narrow pass leaving no path to retreat.

At the column's heart, Daran marched in silence. With every step, the mountain seemed to shift, gravel and shale swirling around him, clinging to his frame. With every yard gained, his changed from that of a man, to a walking mountain. His arms thickened, his back broadened, a massive form carved of stone walked among them. Soldiers whispered as they passed, some in awe, some in fear, but none could deny he was becoming the weapon Anya had promised.

Off to the flank, Tareq moved with a deliberate swagger. He kept his pace
slow, almost theatrical, with his curved swords strapped at his sides and the
scorched antlered skull still perched upon his brow. From his lantern, thin
ribbons of fire licked at the banners on his back. The wings smouldered and
crackled, their edges burned bright, until he looked like a figure cut from a
forgotten legend of Rosk. Soldiers glanced at him as they marched, some
grinning, others making signs of whichever gods they followed, but when he
caught their gaze, he only bared his teeth and let the flames curl higher.

As they rounded a bend in the path, horns blared from the tower above.
Shadows gathered on the walls, the magisters' soldiers and their constructs
waited. Bolts of lightning and fire lanced down from the battlements, crashing
into the narrow trail. Screams echoed between the cliffs as stone shattered, but
still they pressed on.

Tareq broke away, climbing onto a boulder, flames wreathing his body.
"Witness me!" he roared. "I am Tareq, son of Jahlan Sword-Hand! By my
hand you will burn with me this day!"

The archers and magisters turned at once, unleashing volley after volley at
him. Each strike lit the rocks in fire and sparks, but Tareq danced between
them, his swords spinning in wide arcs of flame. The cliff itself seemed to
blaze with his fury, drawing every eye, just as Anya had commanded.

At the column's centre, Daran finally stopped. He planted his feet and raised his arm, and let the mountain answer him. Stones cracked, gravel surged, and with a deep grinding roar, his body continued swelling into colossal proportions. A golem of living rock rose above the army, his arms like siege hammers flexing as the mountain itself rose to answer him.

**

Daran's massive frame surged forward, each step cratering the mountain pass beneath him. As he neared the High Tower gate, he slammed his fists into the ground. The earth responded. Gravel, boulders, and jagged shards of rock twisted upward, forming a towering pillar beneath the gate.

The defenders atop the walls looked on in shock as the massive stone column split the wooden gate in two, lifting it slightly off its hinges. Before they could react, Daran collided with the gate itself. The impact was unimaginable. Planks splintered, metal fittings tore free, and the entire structure exploded inward in a thunderous roar, sending a cloud of dust and splinters across the courtyard.

Soldiers were thrown aside, shields were shattered, and arrows scattered in every direction. The roar of stone grinding against stone echoed off the walls of the pass, and for a heartbeat, the defenders could only stare on in shock. Daran's figure loomed over the broken gates.

The breach had been made, and the High Tower's defenders now faced the full fury of the rebellion.

***

From the walls and tower windows torrents of water surged forth, lances of flame streaked through the air, and forks of lightning cracked down like the fury of the heavens. All of it converged on Daran's massive form. Each impact tore away chunks of stone, dirt crumbled from his shoulders and arms in massive sheets. His earthen body groaned under the punishment, the outer layers exploding into shards with every strike.

Still, he pressed forward. With every step, the ground shook. Fresh soil and rubble dragged up from beneath the cobblestones to knit his form together again. His great arms swung like battering rams, smashing through barricades and crushing any soldiers in his path.

Tareq darted in behind him, swords blazing, wings of smoke trailing. His laughter rising above the chaos as he carved a path, leaving men aflame where they fell.

Anya followed close, her rapier flashing like silver lightning, each thrust finding the narrowest gap in armour. Her precision drew defenders' eyes, giving Tareq the openings to drive deeper into the fray.

Another bolt of lightning slammed into Daran's chest. The entire left side of his stone torso collapsed, rubble spilling freely. Still, he staggered forward, voice booming.

"More! You'll need more than that!"

A wave of fire rolled from the tower's gatehouse, and Tareq shouted for Anya to fall back. But Daran raised what remained of his bulk, shielding them both with his crumbling mass. Flame licked across him, peeling away his outer layers, but once the blast ended, he slammed a colossal fist into the wall, sending rubble cascading down on the defenders above.

The courtyard was in complete chaos now. Rebels surged through the broken gates, the lancers poured in behind them, their wings rattling like thunder as their horses crashed into the enemy. Shatter Tooth warriors came in howling, with their teeth bared, tearing through magister guards with terrifying ferocity.

And still magisters stood on the steps of the High Tower, their robes billowing, weaving death from their staves and hands.

***

The courtyard was a storm of fire, lightning, and the screams of the dying. Daran pressed on, his makeshift body of stone groaned with each step as flames blackened his shoulders and lightning tore chunks away from his chest. Again, and again the ground below surged upward to repair him, but the attacks were relentless.

Then it came.

A high chant rose from the magisters on the steps of the tower. Water essence surged into a single column, compressed into a spear so sharp it cut the air apart with a hiss. It struck Daran solidly. For one breathless instant, his stone form held. Then the beam of water carved cleanly through rock, flesh and bone alike.

Daran's roar shook the mountain. His stone shell collapsed in an avalanche, and his true form tumbled free. As the dust finally cleared, all could see his leg was gone below the knee, his blood freely soaking the dirt.

"No!" Anya cried, her voice breaking and surged forward with her rapier flashing.

But Tareq was already moving. With a furious roar, he charged ahead. With both swords blazed like torches, he struck down the first magister guard who tried to advance on Daran, his blades crossing in a fiery arc that split armour and flesh with ease. Sparks and smoke whipped around him as he pressed forward, the flaming banners trailing behind, giving him the visage of some infernal avenger.

"Come for him, and you'll face me!" Tareq bellowed. His voice carried over the clash, raw with rage.

The magisters hurled another volley of fire and lightning, but Tareq wove through it. His blades spinning, his fury carving open a path toward his friend. Behind him, Anya dropped to her knees beside Daran, pulling her sword belt free as she knelt, securing it to his leg as a makeshift tourniquet to help stop the flow of blood.

Daran's teeth were clenched, his breath ragged. "Finish it," he growled through the pain. "Don't stop for me."

***

The thunder of hooves split the chaos as Boris's winged cavalry crashed into the fray, their banners snapping in the smoke and their lances driving deep into the defender's ranks. The charge swept wide around Daran and Anya, forming a protective wall of steel and horseflesh.

But Tareq was beyond hearing. He was beyond restraint.

His fire had grown wild in answer to his fury. Flames bent unnaturally around his swords, his banners blazed as wings of molten light.

He carved through the magister guard as if they were reeds before a storm. Each stroke of his swords left bodies aflame, armour and flesh melting beneath the searing heat. The air itself seemed to recoil from his presence. Soldiers tried to stand, but none could slow him. Their shields caught fire as his swords struck them, their spears splintered before they reached his chest.

And still he pressed on.

Up the blood-slick steps he stormed, his scream echoing over the mountain as he cut down the defenders one after another. The magisters above wove their spells in panic. Bolts of lightning and sheets of fire slamming against him, but the flames around his body only twisted and grew wilder, feeding on their channelled essence. His fury had made him untouchable.

Tareq burst through the last line of defenders, driving his shoulder into the great oak doors of the High Tower. With a thunderous crack, the fire-wreathed warrior smashed through, wood and iron shattering under his weight. The doors collapsed inward, fire licking along the splintered beams.

He strode into the castle's shadow, swords ablaze, the echo of his challenge rolling through the vaulted hall.

"Magisters!" he roared, his voice thunder itself. "Face your reckoning!"

***

Within the High Tower, the halls were thick with smoke and screams. Tapestries burned as the fire spread from the warrior who stalked through the passages, and the stone walls blackened beneath his passing. Tareq's breath came in harsh growls, each exhale glowed with heat, but still, he did not stop.

The magisters who had once filled these corridors with their quiet dominance, now scrambled like vermin before his fury. Some threw spells in desperation, but their fire and lightning bent to his will, feeding the storm that wrapped around him. Others turned to flee, only for Tareq to hunt them down without hesitation, cutting them down from behind, his blades sinking deeply into their backs with merciless efficiency.

His fury had changed. It was no longer just the desperate wrath of a man

defending his friends or avenging the years of desolation. It was sharper,

hungrier. He laughed as one magister pleaded for mercy, the sound alien, cruel.

"Mercy?" Tareq hissed, driving a flaming blade through the man's chest. "You

never showed us mercy."

The fire spilled across floors and ceilings, it wrapped around beams and

raced up stairwells. The air warped around him, fire no longer answering his

command, instead, he followed its call. His laughter grew harsher, less human.

In the shifting light, his shadow stretched further across the walls, vast and

monstrous. Soldiers fled screaming, both friend and foe.

In his mind's eye, Tareq no longer saw Anya or Daran, or their cause. Only

more fuel for his fire.

At last, through the haze of heat and destruction, Tareq came to a pair of

ornate wooden doors at the end of the hall. They were different from the

others, carved with delicate care, their dark wood polished, untouched by

flame. On their surface gleamed the crest of House Velmira. The silver hawk

on a field of green.

For a heartbeat, he hesitated. Then the fire whispered to him.

... Burn everything....

His fire writhed against the doors, eager to consume them, and Tareq's grip

tightened on his swords. His vision swam between clarity and the rage, between himself and the shadow of something older and crueller, that whispered in the crackling flames.

…Burn it all…

He raised his sword, ready to drive it through the crest of House Velmira, to let the fire consume even this last relic of nobility.

"Tareq."

Her voice pierced through the roar of his fire.

He turned, his one remaining eye glowing from dark flames within, chest heaving, fire still crackling across his arms. Anya stood like a beacon beyond the haze, her rapier drawn but lowered, her eyes fixed on him.

"Look at me," she said.

For a heartbeat, he could not. His breath rasped, the voices in the flames urging him on. To destroy her. She stepped forward, though the heat blistered her skin, and laid a hand against his arm.

…Let nothing remain but ash…

"This is not you," she breathed. "The magisters have hurt us too much. Do not let them take you too."

The fire screamed its protest. Visions poured into him. Great cities aflame, the world scoured clean in flames. He staggered, torn between the hunger of the fire and his emotions.

Anya's voice anchored him. "You are more than this."

Her voice pierced the haze. The laughter died in his throat The whispers faltered. The wings of fire guttered into smoke. With a shudder, his swords dimmed back to steel. He bowed his head, trembling, and Anya caught him before he fell.

Only then did he whisper, hoarse, "I lost myself to the flames."

She steadied him, her hand firm. "You came back to me... to us."

They turned to the crest of House Velmira, and together pushed the doors wide

***

The doors groaned open, and the throne room revealed itself in full, gilded and pristine, as if the ruin of Rosk had never touched it. But Anya and Tareq's breath caught, not at the opulence, but at the figure waiting at the foot of the dais.

Fleshwright Ildran.

His metallic legs clattered against the marble floor, gleaming with cruel precision. The thing they had struck down and left on the collapsing bridge, impossibly alive, its twisted frame reinforced with fresh plates of earthen steel and essence bindings. His pale face was unchanged, smiling and mocking, as if death itself had never dared touch him.

Hatred surged back into Tareq's chest. His grip on his swords tightening until his knuckles whitened. He could hear again the screams of the prisoners in the Blackhold, the clanking of the chains, the rivers of blood. Fear mingled with rage which burned hotter than any fire he had conjured.

Anya froze for only a heartbeat, her rapier rising. But she saw past him.

Three elder magisters flanked him, one robed in fire, another in ice, a third wreathed in storm winds. Their power churned in the air like a brewing tempest. Their eyes locked on the rebels, their contempt as palpable as the weight of their sorcery gathering in the air.

"So, you're still alive…" Tareq spat, voice low and venomous. "I will finish this, once and for all."

Ildran's voice clicked through its metal throat, distorted yet smooth. "You still have no idea what you've done. But soon… you will." His legs hissed as they shifted, the throne room vibrating with the weight of its unnatural gait.

One of the elder magisters sneered, raising a staff that sparked with violet energy. "The pretender has come to die in their master's halls."

Anya stepped forward, her voice ringing across the chamber with a strength she had not known she possessed. "No. This hall will see the end of you. Rosk will be free."

The magisters answered her proclamation with essence. Torrents of fire and ice lanced across the throne room. Tareq roared, his blades igniting once more as he surged to meet them.

***

The first bolt of fire struck the marble floor where Anya had been standing a heartbeat before. She rolled aside, her rapier flashed as she lunged at the caster. Her blade pierced through a shimmering ward, shattering it like glass, and sank deeply into the magister's chest. He gasped, trying to raise a hand for another spell, but Tareq was already upon him. One flaming sword carved down into him, flames spilling across his robes as he crumpled to the floor.

The ice magister answered with a volley of frozen spears. One grazed Anya's arm, her blood spilling warmly down her wrist. Tareq simply batted them aside, the fire surrounding his swords melting them mid-flight. He leapt forward, slamming one blade down, his flames roared as the ice-wielder raised a shield. For a moment, the clash of elements filled the hall. Steam exploded in great plumes, but Tareq pushed through, his second sword slashing across the magister's throat. The man collapsed, his shield unravelling into wisps of steam.

The storm-wielder struck next, sending a fork of lightning screaming across the room. It struck Tareq square in the chest. His body convulsed as the current ran through him. He snarled through the pain, staggering but he did not fall.

Anya darted in, her rapier slashing, but the magister backhanded her with raw essence, sending her crashing into a nearby column. She gasped as the wind was knocked from her lungs, blood dripping from her temple.

"Anya!" Tareq roared, his fury redoubling. He lunged at the lightning-wielder, blades swinging in a whirlwind of fire. Sparks and flame filled the chamber as the magister tried to fend him off the flames with wave after wave of crackling arcs. One strike singed Tareq's shoulder, the smell of burned flesh filling the air, but his momentum did not falter. With a roar, he split the magister's staff in two, then drove a sword straight through the magister's chest, his flames erupting out the other side.

Anya dragged herself back to her feet, her vision spinning. Another magister, robed in green and gold, advanced on her with deadly calm, weaving a spell of binding. Thick, gnarled roots lashed out, wrapping around her wrists and pulling her to her knees. She gritted her teeth, struggling against the bindings, as the magister laughed at her efforts.

Then Tareq's blade pierced through the caster's chest. The spell shattered, the roots dissolving, as Anya thrust upward with her rapier, driving it through the magister's throat. They locked eyes as the man staggered back, grasping at his neck, before collapsing in a heap.

Both rebels staggered, breath ragged, wounds mounting. Still, more magisters waited at the dais, their elemental power gathering. The abomination advanced, his iron legs clattering.

The magisters pressed forward, forcing Anya and Tareq back with walls of flame, torrents of wind, and the relentless clatter of iron legs scraping the marble.

They fought on, blades flashing, spells crashing around them. Each strike bought them ground, but each wound they took stole their strength. Slowly, inexorably, they were being pushed back toward the throne room doors.

The Fleshwright's voice echoed, calm and terrible.
"You cannot win. You will fall, as all rebellions do. Bow before the Tower, and I may yet let you live."

"We will never bow." Tareq spat, though his knees trembled with exhaustion.

Their enemy raised their hands for a final assault, the fight was slipping from Tareq and Anya's grasp. The throne room shook violently.

***

The floor trembled with the aftershock of the collapsing stone, dust and debris raining down as the magister from the Blackhold let out a final, strangled scream beneath the crushing weight. The sickening crunch echoed through the chamber, leaving a brief silence in its wake. At the doorway, Ula emerged, holding Daran upright with ease despite his towering form. The firelight glinted off her sharp teeth as she studied the scene, her eyes alight with approval. "That," she said approvingly, "was a good death."

The remaining magisters recovered from their shock almost immediately, raising their hands to unleash another wave of destruction. A lance of crackling flame streaked through the air, aimed directly at Anya. Her eyes widened as she braced herself for impact, but then something strange happened. The fire veered off course. It twisted and coiled as if it had a mind of its own, drawn like a snake towards Tareq. Sparks spat off the stone floor as the flaming projectile slithered around him, encircling his arms and shoulders without harm.

Tareq's grin widened, a dangerous glint in his eye. He felt the fire obey him, twisting and writhing like a living extension of his fury. He raised both of his twin curved swords high, letting the flames spiral along their edges. With a powerful heave, he hurled them at the air magister. The swords seemed guided by the fire itself, curving through the air with unnatural precision. One blade struck across the magister's shoulder, burning through his robes and scorching the marble beneath him. The other cut a fiery arc along the edge of his cloak, leaving a trail of molten cloth and smoke in its wake.

Anya seized the opening, lunging forward. She sidestepped a desperate counterstrike and struck the magister in a precise motion, her blade piercing the enchanted fabric of his robes. He stumbled backward, blood blossomed through the tear, he crashed into the edge of the dais as the room reverberated with the chaos of battle.

Daran, steadied by Ula, slammed his fist into the floor. The stone erupted into jagged spikes that pinned several magisters where they stood. With a bellow, he swung, sending a wave of debris into the remaining foes, crushing them under the earthen weight of stone. Ula darted in, her blades flashing, cutting through those who struggled free.

Tareq's flames writhed and coiled, a living manifestation of his wrath. The magisters flailed, struggling to regain control as fire, stone, and steel surged around them. Together they pressed forward, the storm turning against its masters.

The High Tower was no longer theirs.

Chapter Sixteen

The chamber was now quiet, the echoes of battle fading into a heavy stillness. Dust still hung in the air, mingling with the faint scent of scorched stone and blood. Anya sat on the throne that had once belonged to her father, her shoulders bowed under the responsibility. Her fingers traced the grooves of the carved armrest, not in command, but in memory.

Around the room, the leaders of her army had gathered, some tending to their wounds, others surveying the aftermath. Their expressions were a mixture of exhaustion, relief, and awe. The bodies of the magisters had been removed, the floor cleared. The high, vaulted ceiling seemed to stretch even higher without the oppressive presence of their foes. For the first time in what felt like an eternity, there was space to breathe.

She exhaled deeply, letting her head fall back against the carved wood. The words that had been unspoken between them all rose in her mind, carried by the silence of the victorious hall. "We have done it," she said softly, her voice carrying over the quiet. The leaders nodded in silent agreement, a collective acknowledgment of their triumph and the cost it had demanded.

For now, the High Tower was theirs. Rosk had been struck a decisive blow, and the magisters' hold had been broken. Yet in that moment, sitting on the throne of her father, Anya allowed herself to be the little girl she once was, and wept.

***

When the tears had passed, Anya straightened, her voice firm despite the weariness she felt through her whole body. "You've all fought beside me through impossible odds," she said, scanning the room. "Now tell me. What do you want from me? What do you plan to do next?"

Ula stepped forward, her posture relaxed but eyes sharp. "My people," she said calmly, "only want to be left alone in the north. To live as we always have, undisturbed by the world below."

Anya leaned forward, her brow furrowing. "You deserve more than that," she said gently, leaning forward. "Your people risked everything, helped destroy the magisters' grip on Rosk. You can live in your lands freely, but you could also shape the future of the north. You could ensure your people are safe without hiding from the world."

Ula's expression didn't change. Her sharp teeth caught the torchlight as she spoke. "We are not like you, Tsarina. We do not want crowns or commands. We honour our goddess, and we honour our way of life. That is enough."

Murmurs rippled through the room, but none interrupted. Anya studied her, respect and disappointment warring in her gaze. "Very well. The north will be yours, undisturbed. But know this, Ula, if your people ever call, or if the magisters rise again, you will find me at your side."

Ula's eyes flicked briefly to Daran and Tareq, then back to Anya. She inclined her head, a silent agreement. "We will hold our lands, Tsarina. And should the need arise, we will fight. But on our terms, not yours."

Anya exhaled, the tension in the throne room loosening ever so slightly. She had respect, and for the Shatter Tooth, that was as much as one could hope for.

Anya leaned back on the throne, letting the quiet settle for a moment before turning her attention to the rest of the gathered leaders. "If Ula has spoken for her people, then I want to hear from the rest of you. What is it you hope to see from this victory?"

Ksiaze Boris stepped forward first, his blue-clad cavalry banners brushing against the stone floor. "The eastern steppes have been bound to the High Tower for far too long, Cousin," he said. His voice was loud and carried authority. "I will see that the people there are free to govern themselves, without interference from whoever sits on the throne. A state of our own. Independent, able to protect their own lands."

Gasps and side-glances flickered among the leaders, but Boris did not waver.

Anya nodded, her eyes narrowed. "And if the magisters or any other tyrant tries to rise again?"

Boris's gaze did not falter. "Then we will fight. The Steppes will never be shackled again. But no distant throne will decide for us again. Our people must choose their own leaders."

Banu spoke quietly but with conviction, his hand brushing the hilt of his curved blade. "My people share Tareq's dream. We will return to the western holds and rebuild them. Fortify them, make them a haven for the oppressed, and ensure the Protectorate is gone from our lands. My people will maintain order, but never impose chains."

One by one, the ambitions of her allies unfolded. Anya listened, her expression unreadable until she finally said, calm and resolute. "Then it is settled. We have freed Rosk from the magister, but that freedom must be guarded. I will act as Tsarina, yes, but I will not rule alone. Together, we will safeguard this land, and the people have a choice in their own fates."

A fragile sense of unity settled over the room. Then Anya turned toward Tareq and Daran, her expression softening. "Everything we've done could never have been achieved without you. Name your reward. Anything within my power."

Tareq exchanged a long, lingering glance with Daran. For a moment, silence stretched across the room, punctuated only by the crackle of the torchlight flickering against the stone walls. Daran finally spoke, his voice calm but resolute. "Our reward, Tsarina, is freedom. To be allowed to choose our own paths when the time comes."

The words struck her harder than any blade. For an instant, she had imagined something else. That Tareq would remain at her side, not only as an ally but as something more. That dream collapsed in her chest.

"You mean… you're leaving?" Her voice cracked sharper than she had intended. "After everything?"

Tareq's gaze did not falter. "I will always come if Rosk calls. But my path is mine to choose. That is all I ask."

Anya's heart pounded in her chest, pride and grief pulling at her, washing over her. She believed there was something more between them, an unbreakable bond forged in fire and blood, but not destined to last.

Daran gave a small, knowing smile, resting a hand on Tareq's shoulder. "The world is wide, Tsarina. Even heroes need the freedom to live their lives how they wish."

Daran shifted, his eyes softer than she'd ever seen them. "I'll remain for a time. I have much to mend. The keep still bears scars from what I unleashed here. Until those are healed, I cannot call myself free."

His words settled like a stone in her chest, heavy but steady. He was offering her more than service, but atonement.

For a long moment, Anya stood silent, her eyes lingering on Tareq. Her hand drifted unconsciously to her stomach, pressing there as if steadying more than just herself. A quiet weight, unspoken but undeniable, tightened her breath. At last, she nodded, jaw tight. "Very well. Go. But know this, High Tower will always welcome you, and I will never forget what you've done."

Tareq dipped his head with a small grin, Daran with a quiet nod. Together they turned and left, their footsteps fading into the stone corridors.

Anya remained alone at the heart of the High Tower. Her hand drifted to the armrest where her father once sat, the carved wood cold beneath her fingers. The crown on her brow seemed heavier with every breath, pressing her into the seat as though the throne itself meant to claim her.

She had won a kingdom. Yet in that moment, she felt smaller than ever, a single spark flickering in a vast, dark hall.

Chapter Seventeen

A soft breeze drifted through the open windows, ruffling Sokol's dark feathers as he preened atop Anya's arm. She traced the lines of his wings absently, her thoughts drifting over the battles and years that had carried her here. The High Tower had become more than a seat of power. It was a haven for the people of Rosk, and this turret chamber was her own small refuge.

The scent of fresh straw mixed with the faint tang of bird feathers, which softened the polished stone walls. Here, Anya could breathe, if only for a moment. Without the weight of the crown pressing down on her shoulders. Without small hands tugging at her sleeve, begging her not to let go.

Sokol let out a soft trill, turning his head to look at her with bright, intelligent eyes. Anya smiled, feeling a rare spark of warmth in her chest. It was moments like this that reminded her she was still human beneath the title of Tsarina. She could close the door to the rest of the world, to politics, to rebellions and wars, and simply exist, if only for a little while.

Outside, the wind carried the distant sounds of life in the tower, footsteps, laughter, and the occasional clatter of metal from the armoury, but inside this room, it was a sanctuary. For a brief moment, she allowed herself to just be Anya, not the Tsarina, not a commander, not the symbol of rebellion, just a woman with a bird on her arm.

The floor beneath Anya shuddered violently, sending a jolt through her chest and stomach. The heavy wooden beams of the High Tower groaned as if protesting the force beneath them. Dust cascaded from the rafters and into the air of the room, settling in fine clouds that caught the light of the early morning sun. A low, resonant rumbling rolled across the land from the west, deep and steady. It reverberated in her bones, rattling the windows and sending a warning pulse through the tower walls.

Her heart leapt into her throat. Instinctively, she bolted toward the nearest window, leaning out into the chill morning air. Her gaze swept across the horizon, scanning the distant hills and plains. Smoke. Thick, black plumes of smoke clawed at the sky in twisting plumes from the west, blotting out the morning sun. Smoke from a burning field or village shouldn't be so visible from this far away.

Her stomach dropped as she understood. The Blackhold. The ruined prison, steeped in untold horror and dark experiments best forgotten. The realisation hit her like a physical blow, leaving her breathless. Had it begun again? Had someone taken advantage of the chaos to rebuild it, or had it been disturbed from its ashes? Her mind raced, thinking of all she had fought for, all she had seen destroyed, and the fragile sense of peace she had carved out over the past year for her people, and for her young family.

Sokol flapped nervously against the window frame, sensing the tension. His shrill cry pierced the eerie quiet that had followed the tremors. Anya's hands tightened on the wooden sill, her knuckles white as her gaze stayed fixed on the western horizon. Flames flickered in the smoke, though she could not yet make out if they were fire or some unnatural glow.

The tremors subsided, leaving a heavy silence in their wake. But the plume of smoke remained. Stubborn and foreboding, it was a grim beacon on the distant landscape. For a moment, Anya felt the weight of the world pressing on her shoulders, heavier than any crown or title she had borne. The quiet before the storm was complete, and yet the warning in the air was unmistakable. The Blackhold had risen again.

***

Far to the south, the rhythmic hammering of Daran's forge faltered, the sound of hammer striking metal replaced by the deep, resonant vibration that shivered through the ground beneath him. Sparks from the fire flickered and danced unevenly, disturbed by the subtle quiver in the floor. He froze, his senses sharpening as the rumbling continued, deeper and more insistent than any tremor he had felt in recent memory.

He lowered himself to his knees, letting the weight of his body press against the hard stone floor. His prosthetic arm, now an unassuming and unadorned tool, hovered above the surface, fingers splayed as he tried to reach out beyond the material, seeking the source of the disturbance. The pulse he felt was vast and wild, unlike any natural earthquake or the echoes of battle he had known. It was alive and deliberate. Malice hummed through it all like a voice.

Sweat pricked at his brow as he focused, willing his senses to pierce the distance between him and the western horizon. The dark presence called to him across the lands of Rosk, distant but unmistakable. It was coming from the ruins of Blackhold. Memories of their battle for freedom and the price they had paid surged within him, making his chest tighten.

He gritted his teeth and slowly rose to his feet while still keeping his gaze toward the northwest. His forge seemed smaller, the hammers and anvils trivial against the weight of what he felt. The simple prosthetic leg beneath him, a reminder of the life he had tried to reclaim for himself, felt both grounding and insufficient.

Daran's jaw tightened. He clenched his fist, feeling the earth beneath him hum and shift as if acknowledging his presence. Somewhere far away, the source of the tremors waited. The call was unmistakable. Blackhold was stirring again, and he knew that soon, he would have to leave the quiet of his forge to confront whatever stirred in the west.

***

Tareq hit the ground hard, the soil beneath him shuddering violently. He struggled to his hands and knees, coughing as fine ash and grit stung his eyes and filled his lungs. The smell of burning stone and charred timber was thick in the air, carrying a bitter tang that made his stomach turn.

All around him, the fields they had tilled were covered in a black dusting, the young shoots of crops bending and breaking beneath the weight. The wooden fences of his property groaned and splintered as the tremors rippled through the land, and the nearby houses shuddered on their foundations. Shouts of alarm and fear echoed from every direction as villagers scrambled, some tripping over the debris-littered ground, others clutching children and livestock, trying to escape the sudden onslaught of ash and dust.

Tareq struggled to his feet, his body aching from the sudden throw, and shielded his eyes against the choking clouds that swirled above. The dark plume from the Blackhold rose impossibly high, black and crimson streaked with flickering sparks of fire. The sheer scale of it was overwhelming, dwarfing the landscape, blotting out the sun, and casting a crimson haze across the horizon.

His heart pounded as he realised the eruption wasn't a natural calamity. This was deliberate, the destructive energy of the magisters unleashed once again. He could see the villagers, some frozen in shock, others fleeing blindly, and knew that they would need his protection.

Ash settled on everything, coating his hair, his clothes, and the rich brown soil of his fields. The world seemed to tilt around him as tremors shook the ground in a constant, uneven rhythm. Tareq gritted his teeth, his mind racing. The Blackhold was alive again, and this time the devastation was spilling far beyond its walls.

He took a deep breath, tasting smoke and fire in his mouth, and rose fully to his feet. He could no longer wait. The rebellion, his friends, and all the innocent lives in Rosk were in peril. With one glance toward the western horizon, where the plume of the Blackhold loomed like a dark mountain.

Chapter Eighteen

The western holds had become a nightmarish wasteland. Villages smouldered in ruin, smoke rising from shattered homes and fields stripped to blackened ash. The rivers ran thick with mud and blood, and the forests were scorched where the strange abominations had passed. Survivors moved like shadows, constantly on the lookout, their eyes wide with fear, clutching what weapons they could find.

Towering and twisted, obsidian flesh glinting, their movements too graceful for things so monstrous. Shards of gemstone jutted from their torsos, each glowing with a different elemental hunger. Ruby-red burned barns from afar, emerald-green tangled forests into killing snares, pale blue froze men to brittle statues. They hunted with unnatural precision, as though commanded by a mind too vast and cruel to see.

Even the Flying Stags, veterans of endless campaigns, found their weapons shattering uselessly against obsidian hide. The villages rebuilt in defiance of the magisters were already graveyards again, the screams of their people carried on the wind.

The people who survived whispered rumours of something far worse than the magisters' rule. The horrors were only the first wave, and they seemed to grow stronger the longer the eruption continued. The villagers spoke of faintly glowing eyes and crystals through the ash seeing where no one should, of elemental forces bending to the creatures' will, and of the way the land itself seemed to twist in response to them. Fear, despair, and rage mingled together, leaving only one thought on every survivor's mind. If this was the final strategy of the magisters, nothing would ever be safe again in Rosk.

***

Tareq's boots skidded across the ash-covered ground, leaving shallow furrows as he circled the obsidian-skinned creature. Each of his twin blades traced arcs of fire through the smoke, their sparks illuminating the jagged shards embedded in the monster's skin. It was smaller than some horrors that had emerged, roughly the size of a man, but its unnatural strength was immediately apparent. When Tareq lunged, the creature's arm whipped out with a speed that belied its bulk, blocking the fiery arcs with its jagged arm.

The impact sent a shockwave through Tareq's arms, forcing him to stumble back a few steps to regain his balance.

The monster responded with a brutal counterattack, swinging a clawed hand toward Tareq's head. He rolled under the blow, the heat from his blades sizzling against the ashen ground, but the force threw him harshly to one knee. Dust filled his lungs as he struggled to rise, feeling the raw elemental energy emanating from the shards embedded in the creature's body.

Tareq gritted his teeth and lunged again, aiming for a weak spot where two shards jutted awkwardly from its shoulder. His blade bit into the blackened skin, scraping along the edge of the rock, and he felt a sting as the shards cracked slightly under the force. The creature roared, a soundless wail that rattled his ears and caused the ground to tremble beneath him. Its other arm lashed out, knocking one of his swords from his grip, sparks flying as it skittered across the furrowed ground.

With his remaining blade, Tareq danced backward, narrowly avoiding another strike that sent a plume of ash and dirt into the air. Each attack from the monster was unpredictable, powered by the strange elemental shards in its body, and Tareq had to use every ounce of skill and speed to stay ahead. The creature lunged again, faster than before, its obsidian skin glinting in the firelight, and Tareq knew that one mistake could be fatal. It was then, at that moment before the deadly strike connected, that the massive boulder arced through the air, crashing into the creature.

Tareq scrambled to regain his footing. His chest heaved as he wiped a smear of soot from his cheek. The creature lurched to its feet, shards of multi-coloured rock embedded in its flesh, its body twisting unnaturally as the massive boulder had struck. The impact had sent cracks splitting across the blackened surface of its torso, and molten streaks began seeping from the wounds.

Tareq's mind raced, adrenaline sharpening his senses. The creature's glowing eyes snapped toward him, and it let out a grating shriek that reverberated through the air. Its clawed hands struck at the ground, sending tremors through the charred soil as it struggled to rise. Tareq rolled to the side, narrowly avoiding a swing of its jagged arm, feeling the heat of its elemental shards as they sparked against the ground.

From the haze, a shadow surged forward, a hulking figure of stone and dirt, its limbs moving with measured power. With a stomp, it lifted another enormous boulder and flung it like a meteor. It collided with the creature again, pulverizing the remaining shards in its chest and sending it tumbling backward. Tareq let out a sharp breath, relief mingling with the pounding of his heart, and then readied his blade once more, flames licking up his arms.

Tareq went over to pick up his dropped sword, letting out a bark of laughter despite the surrounding chaos. "I was wondering when you'd get here," he called, flicking sparks from his swords with a casual twist.

Daran's eyes flicked to the horizon, where smoke still swirled over the Blackhold. "I didn't come alone," he said, his voice steady even as dust clung to his clothes. "I met up with some of Anya's forces along the way. They brought a message for us."

Tareq leaned on his blades, his curiosity piqued. "A message from who? And don't tell me it's just orders to fight."

"No," Daran replied, hefting the boulder he'd just used to crush the horrors. "They went through the archives the Protectorate left behind. And they finally figured out what they were really trying to achieve."

Tareq raised an eyebrow, fire flickering across the blade in his hands. "Enlighten me. Should I be ready to hate them even more?"

Daran shook his head, his jaw tight. "The Blackhold wasn't just a prison. For all their cruelty, suffering and death, the magisters were trying to build a bulwark." He let the words hang as he studied Tareq's face, ensuring the weight of his revelation settled in. "The magisters were preparing for the return of the Fallen Gods, as they called them. What they did to us and the others, they were meant to create a force capable of defending Rosk from what is coming."

Tareq's laughter faltered, replaced by a slow, thoughtful hum. "So, all that suffering... all the people we fought to free from the magister's horrors... they were making soldiers to save the continent?"

Daran nodded grimly. "Yes. They were creating warriors capable of standing against forces far greater than even the magi and their guards could manage. They were trying to hold the breach."

Tareq spat a little on the ground, shaking his head in disbelief. "And we've been fighting back against them to restore order, and by doing so, caused all of this to happen. We tore it all down, and now the world burns."

Daran's gaze drifted back toward the smoking ruins of the Blackhold. "It doesn't excuse what they've done. But now we know why the magisters acted as they did. Now we have a greater purpose, what we were made for."

Tareq's eyes glinted, fire reflected in their depths. "Purpose, eh?"

Daran allowed a brief smirk, clapping Tareq on the shoulder. "Let's end this. For good."

***

The ground shuddered again, this time not from the earth itself but from the pounding of clawed feet. From the ashen haze toward the coast, several smaller horrors came loping forward, four-limbed, twisted things with obsidian flesh stretched too tightly over their frames. Their eyeless faces turned toward the two men as if drawn to the heat of their breath, the gems jutting from their bodies glowing faintly with eerie colours.

Tareq spun his swords in his hands, taking a defensive guard. "Looks like we've got company."

Daran shifted his stance, gripping a jagged length of stone he'd torn from the ground. "Any idea how to kill these things? Or do we just keep smashing until they stop moving?"

"Not quite," Tareq said, breaking into a grim grin as the creatures closed in. "They're tougher than they look. Cut them apart, and they'll crawl right back together. The trick is their gems. Those rocks sticking out of their skin. Each one's an anchor. Shatter them, and the body goes with it."

The nearest monster lunged, its body twisting unnaturally mid-leap. Tareq stepped into it, his twin blades flashing. He slashed low, then high, carving arcs of fire through the ash-thick air. The strike missed the creature's head, but one blade caught a jagged emerald shard protruding from its ribs. The crystal cracked, and the monster shrieked soundlessly before collapsing into blackened dust.

"Like that!" Tareq barked, kicking the remains away as he turned to face the next.

Another horror darted toward Daran, its limbs flailing with uncanny speed. Daran planted his good foot firmly in the earth, then drove his stone arm forward like a spear. The impact caught the creature in the chest, but instead of driving it back, the thing wrapped its limbs around the stone, dragging itself closer. With a snarl, Daran twisted, forcing the monster sideways until his arm scraped against a glowing sapphire spike near its shoulder. The shard cracked, and the monster convulsed before going limp, sagging off his weapon and crumbling into ash.

"They make a lot of noise when they die," Daran muttered, shaking dust from his hands.

"Better than not dying at all," Tareq shot back, his blades flashing again as he intercepted two more rushing forms. He ducked low, spun, and his swords carved large trails of flame across the nearest one's chest. A ruby shard split, and the beast burst into fragments.

Daran ripped another boulder from the earth with a sharp gesture of his hand, hurling it into a pair that were circling around Tareq. The stone smashed one flat, but the other kept moving, claws scraping across the ground as it closed the distance.

"They're relentless," Daran growled, stepping back into formation beside Tareq.

"Good," Tareq replied, teeth bared in a feral grin as he spun his swords into ready stance. "That means you won't run out of practice targets anytime soon."

The clash of steel and stone and skin stopped at once. Both men froze as the air itself seemed to thicken, their lungs struggling for breath. Then it came, low and thunderous, not carried on the wind or from any mouth, but driven into their minds.

...You are mere sparks in the void...

The words were not spoken so much as forced against the very insides of their skulls. Tareq's knees buckled first. His blades slipped from his hands, clattering to the ash-strewn earth as he clutched at his head, teeth gritted against the crushing weight. Daran stumbled a step before crumpling beside him, his stone shell started to fall apart.

The ground itself trembled in rhythm with the voice, as though the land was echoing its immense will. Their vision swam, firelight and shadow twisting unnaturally around them.

Tareq slammed his fist into the dirt, his voice hoarse, trying to force defiance past the weight bearing down on him. "Get... out of my head!"

But the pressure only grew. Their bones felt as though they would shatter. Daran slammed his palm against the ground, trying to ground himself, to feel the earth as he always had, but even that was drowned beneath the voice. His heart pounded so loudly he thought it might burst.

...Flesh against stone, ash against the tide...

Tareq groaned, forcing himself up onto one knee, though every muscle screamed against it. He turned his head toward Daran, his eyes narrowed against the crushing weight.

"Daran..." he gasped through clenched teeth. "You... feel that?"

...We endure, we return, we rise...

Daran's jaw was tight, his face pale with strain, but his eyes burned with understanding and fear. "A Fallen God," he rasped. "It's speaking to us."

And all around them, more twisted silhouettes emerged through the ash.

***

The ground shook with a thunderous impact that forced the air from their lungs. Tareq and Daran lifted their heads, straining against the weight of the unseen voice, and saw it descend through the dark clouds.

A massive creature had slammed into the earth, sending cracks racing like lightning through the blackened soil. It was easily three times the height of a man, its hulking frame a shifting kaleidoscope of colour. Great wings unfurled behind it, not of feather or flesh, but vast sheets of elemental energy that rippled and burned, flashing in violent hues of fire, water, lightning, and earth. Each beat of its wings sent waves of hot wind and shards of ash whipping across the battlefield.

Its entire body was studded with jagged gems, hundreds of them, each pulsing with different colours and rhythm.

Massive horns curled forward from its skull, jagged like volcanic rock, glowing faintly with veins of inner fire. As it raised one colossal arm, the air shimmered and warped in its grip, the ash in the air drawn inwards. In an instant, a massive sword formed out of nothingness, its blade impossibly wide, crackling with multiple elements. Fire licked along one edge, water dripped and steamed along the other, lightning coursed down the fuller, and stone encased the hilt like unbreakable armour.

The pressure of the voice deepened, and though its maw never opened, its intent bled into their minds.

.... *Bow.... Or break....*

All around, the smaller horrors that had been charging moments before stopped in their tracks. They skittered backward, lowering their twisted forms as if in reverence. Their shards dimmed, their aggression was gone, replaced with obedience. It was as though the towering being's mere presence had overridden their every instinct.

Tareq struggled to his feet, twin blades blazing weakly in his hands, his body trembling with strain and awe. He forced a smirk, though it was thin and bitter. "Well... Daran... you were right. I think that might be a Fallen God."

Daran's prosthetic hand clenched into a fist. His jaw was tight as he stared

up at the being. His voice was grim, heavy with the weight of understanding.

"And it doesn't want to kill just us…"

The ground trembled as the creature stepped forward, each footfall impacting

the scorched earth like thunder. Tareq and Daran barely had a moment to ready

themselves before the massive sword swung down, the force splitting the

ground and sending a shockwave of ash and stone roaring outward.

Tareq dove to the side, rolling across the blackened soil as the blade

slammed into the ground where he had stood. The impact sent him sprawling,

his ears ringing, his lungs burned with dust. He forced himself up, fire licking

along his blades, and sprinted toward the godspawn's leg. With a cry, he

slashed twice in quick arcs, sparks bursting where his blades met the creature's

gemstone-studded hide.

But the gems were like solid steel. His blades skittered across them, leaving

only faint scorch marks.

The monster moved with terrifying speed for its size. One of its great wings

swept outward like a storm, and the force caught Tareq full in the chest,

hurling him across the battlefield. He slammed into the dirt with a grunt, the

fire of his blades flickering weakly.

"Keep it busy!" Daran shouted. He raised his prosthetic, and the earth

answered. Stones ripped themselves from the ground, orbiting him in jagged clusters before he launched them in a storm at the giant's chest. A few shattered against the glowing gems, but one struck a crack already forming near its shoulder, splintering a shard of violet crystal. The beast let out a soundless roar that echoed in their minds, a wave of raw pain and fury that nearly knocked them both senseless.

It paid them back with interest. The sword lifted, and fire erupted from its edge, a wave of molten flame sweeping across the battlefield. Daran raised walls of stone to shield them, but the heat seared through, and one wall burst apart under the force, throwing him to his knees.

Tareq staggered up, coughing blood, his blades reigniting. He darted forward, slipping past the sweep of the sword, his body a blur, barely visible against the glowing blade. He leapt onto the godspawn's leg, stabbing one blade deep into the gaps between its armour-like hide. With a roar of effort, he pulled himself upward, climbing the creature like a burning vine.

The monster's hand came up, massive and crackling with lightning, trying to swat him away. Tareq launched himself higher, stabbing his second blade into a glowing gem just below the collarbone. This time, the strike hit true. The gem cracked, exploding in a burst of white-blue sparks. The godspawn staggered, its body writhing with uncontrolled energy.

"Daran, now!" Tareq bellowed.

Daran, bleeding from a cut across his face, slammed both hands to the ground. The earth split, and a jagged spike of stone erupted from beneath the creature's knee. The force toppled the giant backward, its wings flaring wildly, sending storms of fire, ice, and lightning into the air.

Tareq clung to its chest as it fell, the impact rattling his bones. He drove his blade down again, trying to shatter another gem, but the monster's hand closed around him. He screamed as the pressure crushed his ribs, the fire of his blades sputtering under the weight of its grip.

Daran roared, lifting boulders with every shred of his strength, hurling them at the creature's face, trying to free his friend. One shattered against its horn, another cracked a gem near its jaw, but the godspawn's grip only tightened.

Through the burning in his chest, Tareq forced his fire to surge, his swords blazed white hot. "Daran!" he gasped. "Take out the gems! Break them all!"

Daran's eyes widened with horror. "Not without you!"

But the godspawn's thoughts crashed into both their minds, deeper and darker than ever.

...We were before your kind... and we will remain...

Tareq gave him a wide grin, despite the pain.

And the hand squeezed harder.

***

The godspawn's grip tightened until bones finally gave way. A sickening crunch echoed across the battlefield, and Tareq's cry was cut short. The monster dropped him like a broken glass, his body hitting the ground with a thud, all his flames extinguished.

Before Daran could even reach him, the creature's massive foot came down, stamping the ground, with Tareq beneath it, into dust and ruin. The impact sent a shockwave tearing outward, flattening the last remnants of the nearby buildings, turning the earth black with molten cracks.

For a heartbeat, silence followed. Daran stared, his chest heaving, his vision blurring.

"No…" His voice broke, low and shaking. His hand dug into the ash, clutching at nothing. "Not like this."

Something inside him snapped.

The surrounding ground quaked violently as if responding to his grief and rage. Stones tore themselves free from the soil, pulled by an unseen gravity, swirling in a storm around him. His skin split and bled, but instead of flowing freely, the blood hardened into black earth, forming jagged plates across his flesh. His eyes glowed like molten rock, burning brighter with every heartbeat.

"I will stop you!" Daran roared, his voice shaking the very land.

The battlefield itself seemed to answer him. The plain buckled and rose, a mountain growing in seconds, its peak forming into his shape. His body stretched higher and higher, absorbing boulders, trees, and shattered earth, until he stood as a colossal earthen titan, nearly equal in height to the godspawn. Wings of stone unfurled from his back, jagged and crude but mighty. His prosthetic arm transformed into a spire of sharpened rock, a weapon as long as a siege tower. His missing leg reformed from molten earth, solid and unbreakable.

The godspawn turned toward him. Its massive head tilting, the gems flashing in a kaleidoscope of cruel colours. It raised its blade of raw creation, but this time, it faced something closer to its equal.

Daran slammed a colossal fist into the ground, sending a wave of spikes rushing toward the godspawn's feet. The creature staggered back, its wings beating furiously, but Daran pressed forward, each step making the earth quake.

"You took my brother," Daran bellowed, his voice echoing across the plains like an avatar of rage and war. "You might be a god, but now you die."

The godspawn came at him, faster than something so huge should have been able to move. Its elemental blade swept in a wide arc, a rainbow of destructive light trailing in its wake. Daran raised both massive arms and caught the strike, the impact blasting chunks of stone from his body. The shockwave split the ground between them like a canyon, but he held fast.

With a roar, he shoved back. The sword's edge screeched against his rockbound limbs, sparks and shards flying. Before the creature could pull its blade back, Daran swung a fist the size of a carriage into its head. The blow landed with a thunderous crack, sending the godspawn reeling, its wings thrashing to steady itself.

But the creature retaliated instantly. The gems across its body flared one after the other. Blades of raw magic shot out in every direction, tearing into Daran's stone flesh, gouging holes through his colossal form. He staggered backwards, but refused to fall.

He stomped his foot, and the land obeyed. A wall of jagged stone surged upward, catching a barrage of flame before it could incinerate him. With his other hand, he reached down and ripped a slab of rock from the earth, moulding it into a crude hammer.

Daran growled, swinging the hammer in a crushing arc.

It slammed into the godspawn's torso, shattering several glowing gems. The monster howled, an ear-splitting, otherworldly screech, as shards of fractured crystal burst outward. Smoke and light poured from the cracks in its body like bleeding fire.

The creature lunged, driving its sword through Daran's side. Rock shattered, molten cracks splitting open, yet he did not retreat. He clamped both hands on the blade, holding it inside his stone body, anchoring the godspawn in place.

With the last of his strength, Daran pulled the creature down to him. "For Tareq."

The ground beneath them split apart as he drew every ounce of earth and stone from deep below. His titan body swelled, towering even higher, arms glowing with molten veins of fury. He lifted the godspawn overhead, struggling as the creature writhed and lashed with its wings, sparks and fire blasting against his form.

With a roar that shook the skies, Daran brought it down. He slammed the godspawn into the earth. Once, twice, three times, until the ground itself cratered beneath the blows. On the final strike, he drove his molten fist deep into the creature's chest, crushing the largest gem embedded there.

The gem shattered like glass, releasing a torrent of energy that burst outward in a storm of fire, wind, and lightning. The godspawn let out its last scream before collapsing into a heap of broken crystal and withered flesh, its massive sword dissolving into smoke.

Daran stood over the ruined husk, his colossal body crumbling as the power that sustained it bled away. Piece by piece, the stone fell from him, until he was left kneeling in his mortal form, chest heaving, blood running freely.

He looked over at where Tareq's broken body lay in the ash. His fists clenched, and his head bowed.

"It's done, brother. It's done."

***

The army slowed its march as the lone figure stumbled into view through the haze of ash and smoke. Soldiers shifted uneasily, hands tightening on weapons, some even raising them defensively. Something about the man's shape, the limp in his stride, told Anya before she could make out his face clearly.

"Daran," she whispered, already sliding from her saddle.

She ran to him, her cloak streaming behind her, dust rising with every step. He looked broken, his skin scorched, clothes torn and blackened with soot, his right arm wrapped tight around his side where blood seeped through the cloth. Yet he was still alive.

When she reached him, she threw her arms around him. For a moment he stood still, as though the strength to even return the gesture had left him. But then he held her back, a weary, trembling embrace.

Relief flooded her chest, but only for an instant. She pulled away quickly, her eyes darting past him, scanning the battlefield, the ruined coast, the smoke still curling up into the sky. "Where is he?" she asked. "Where is Tareq?"

Daran said nothing. His mouth opened, then shut again, his jaw tightening. His gaze fell to the ground.

"No…" Anya's voice broke. "Daran, no. Tell me he's here. Tell me he's behind you."

Still silent, Daran reached into his cloak. His hand shook as he withdrew a charred, misshapen piece of earthen steel. The mask he had once forged for Tareq. Its surface was cracked, warped by heat and battle. He placed it in her hands, his eyes heavy with grief.

"I'm sorry, Anya," he whispered, his voice hoarse.

Anya shook her head, denial breaking her voice. "No. He's out there. He has to be. We'll… We'll find him."

Her words faltered as her fingers traced the ruined steel. Her knees gave way, and ash fell with her tears.

Her words faltered as her fingers traced the ruined steel. Her chest tightened, her throat closing with the weight of the truth. Her knees gave way, and ash fell with her tears. The soldiers behind her stood silent, watching their Tsarina crumble as the ash continued to fall around them.

Daran continued walking and did not look back.

Epilogue

The tavern was thick with the smell of smoke, sweat, and old ale. The hearth fire crackled weakly, its flames barely pushing back the chill that clung to Kul Vazhen at this time of year. When the door swung open, a gust of cold air followed the two figures in, stirring the smoke across the rafters.

The chatter stopped. Dice hands froze mid-roll. Tankards paused in the air. Visitors were rare in Kul Vazhen, rarer still during the bitter months when the roads iced and only fools or desperate souls travelled.

The pair moved in step, cloaks dusted with ash and dirt. The shorter one was broad, squat, his gait heavy like someone used to bearing weight. The taller of the two was lean, his movements fluid, almost too smooth for the rough surroundings. Their boots thudded against the wooden floor as every pair of eyes in the tavern followed them.

They reached the bar, where the barkeep stood polishing a pewter mug he had been holding since they entered. He squinted up at them, suspicion in his gaze.

The taller figure lowered his hood. A young man was revealed beneath, his eyes sharp with travel and determination, auburn hair tied back in a tight ponytail. His voice cut through the silence.

"We're looking for the master smith. Where can we find him?"

The barkeep's hand stilled. For a heartbeat, no one moved. Then the murmurs began again, low and wary, as though the tavern itself was unsettled by the question.

The barkeep leaned forward slowly. "Depends on who's asking. And what business they've got with him."

The shorter of the pair let a heavy purse fall onto the counter with a thud that silenced the low murmur of the tavern. The weight of it spoke louder than words, the coins inside shifting with a metallic clink that turned more than a few heads. The man's thick, calloused hand lingered atop it for a moment, daring anyone nearby to think of trying their luck.

When he finally spoke, his voice rolled like gravel down a hill, thick with an accent that bent the words until they were almost foreign. "Payin' customers are askin', aye? An' these payin' customers'll be wantin' a round. Somethin' strong. Somethin' warmin'. We've been walkin' long miles in worse weather

than this."

The barkeep, a tall, gaunt man with thinning hair, studied the stranger with

wary eyes. A few of the regulars leaned back in their chairs, casting sideways

glances at one another. The air was suddenly thick with curiosity.

The stocky traveller gave a grin beneath his hood, the faint gleam of teeth

flashing in the firelight. He nudged the purse across the counter with two

fingers, the gesture casual, but there was something pointed in the way he did

it. "So then," he rumbled, "ye'll not be keepin' us thirsty, eh? We've gold

enough t' drown half this bloody town, an' bellies too empty t' argue with

parched throats."

The barkeep finally reached for a pair of mugs, though his eyes never left the

stranger's face. The room itself seemed to tilt toward the bar, every ear

straining to catch the exchange, every drink paused halfway to lips. The shorter

man lifted his chin, his heavy cloak shifting, showing the outline of arms thick

as tree trunks beneath it.

"Drinks first," he growled, his voice carrying a hard edge now. "Questions

after. That's how business is done."

As soon as the barkeep slid the frothing mugs onto the scarred bar top, the

shorter man snatched one up in his thick hands and tipped it back in a single

pull. Foam and ale spilled down into the mass of his immense, brown beard, streaking it damp. He let out a satisfied grunt, slammed the mug back onto the wood hard enough to rattle the rest, and fixed the barkeep with a pointed stare.

"Now then," he growled, his words thick with a heavy, rolling accent that carried the sound of stone and surf, "where's th' master smith?."

Before the barkeep could stammer a reply, the crowd's attention shifted. From a shadowed corner near the hearth, an elderly figure rose slowly to his feet. His skin was deep and dark, weathered like old oak, his long beard bound tightly, his white hair woven with simple braids that swung as he moved. He leaned heavily on a crutch, each step deliberate, the thud of wood-on-wood echoing louder in the silence that had fallen over the tavern.

The old man's eyes, sharp despite the weight of years, settled on the cloaked pair at the bar.

"You'll find no smith worth your coin here," he rasped, his voice carrying authority even through its gravel. "Only an old man who's seen too many winters… unless it's me you've come lookin' for."

The shorter man wiped the ale from his beard with the back of his hand, then straightened with surprising dignity for someone so stout. He thrust forward a calloused hand, scarred and ringed with iron bands around thick fingers.

"Falden Rockbreaker," he declared in that gravel-thick accent, his voice carrying through the tavern like a hammer striking an anvil. "At yer service.

An' this lad here's wi' me. Now…" he squinted at the elder with a flicker of recognition, "Would ye be Master Boranson?"

The old man halted mid-step, his white braids swaying slightly as he leaned on the crutch. His eyes narrowed, and for a long moment he did not move. Then, with a weary sigh that seemed to carry a lifetime of burdens, he gave the smallest of nods.

"I am he," he muttered, his voice low and tired, as though even admitting it took something from him. "Though that name's near as forgotten."

Falden's expression softened for the briefest instant, then hardened again with purpose. He cast a glance at the crowded tavern, the watching eyes, the ears too eager for gossip. Then he leaned forward, lowering his voice but not losing the weight of command in it.

"We need t'talk, master smith. Me an' the boy both. But not here, wi' all these gawkers hangin' on every word. Somewhere quiet. Somewhere we won't be overheard."

The younger man at his side said nothing, only lifted his mug to his lips and let his sharp eyes sweep across the room, watching every reaction in silence.

Boranson's crutch tapped once against the floorboards. The old man studied them for a long moment, his dark face unreadable, then jerked his chin toward a table at the back of the tavern.

Falden thumped the counter with two thick fingers and called out to the barkeep in his rolling accent.

"More ales, lad, six this time. We'll need the drink for the words I've tae say."

The barkeep muttered something about ungrateful travellers but fetched the mugs all the same. Falden swept three of them into his arms before the foam even settled, leaving the rest for the boy to carry. With mugs in hand, the pair followed Boranson as he shuffled through the smoky taproom, his crutch thumping against the boards in slow, deliberate rhythm. Eyes tracked them as they passed until the old smith pushed open a warped door that led into a quieter chamber at the back.

***

It was warmer here, the smell of soot and iron clinging to the walls, though the forge lay cold for now. A long bench and rough-hewn table sat beneath a guttering lantern. Boranson lowered himself with a grunt, setting his crutch aside, while Falden and the boy slid onto the bench opposite.

Falden raised his mug in a brief salute before downing half of it in one go. Foam clung to his moustache as he slammed it onto the table with a hollow thud.

"We need yer help, smith," he began, leaning forward, the weight of his words heavy despite the roughness of his tone. "I'm no' here by chance. I'm an emissary, sent from across the sea. My kin, my people, they've felt it. Same as ye. The Breach o' the Fallen Gods."

Boranson stiffened, his weathered eyes hardening as if struck.

Falden pressed on, his voice lowering. "They told me the tale. How ye faced one of the godspawn yerself. How ye cut it down wi' yer bare strength, then pulled the wound in the world shut, an' dragged the whole cursed breach beneath ocean an' stone. It shook the earth so hard we felt it even across the waters."

He spread his hands, thick fingers splayed wide. "But my folk... we're facin' the same. Another breach is risin'. Another spawn clawing its way free. An' we're no' strong enough t' bury it alone. We've got brave souls, aye, but no one with the power ye wield. We need ye, Boranson. Without ye, my people'll be swept into fire an' darkness."

The young man beside Falden remained silent, only sipping from his mug, though his eyes flicked from Falden to Boranson, measuring every reaction with quiet intensity.

Boranson exhaled slowly, his broad chest rising and falling. The hand gripping his mug trembled slightly. When he finally spoke, it was hoarse, weary, but with a steel edge buried deep beneath.

"I'm too old, Rockbreaker," he said at last, his voice heavy as iron. "Too old and too broken. My bones ache with every step, my hands fail me when I grip a hammer. I didn't do it alone last time. There was someone else… Stronger, younger, braver. I only played my part."

He gave a bitter smile that carried no mirth. "The world took its due from me for what I did. I've nothing left to give."

Falden leaned forward, his dark eyes softening. His voice lost some of its bluster, carrying a note of quiet understanding.

"Aye, I believe ye. I can see the years on ye, plain as the scars. But broken or no', Boranson, ye're still the one who stood where no one else would. Ye've still got somethin' my folk need. Even if it's no' yer hammer arm, it's the wisdom o' what ye learned standin' against them."

He glanced at the boy, then gave him a small nod. "Show him."

The boy, who had been silent until now, set down his half-finished mug and pulled a satchel from his shoulder. From it, he drew a fine bundle of cloth, bound tight. He laid it carefully on the table between them and, with slow, deliberate hands, unwrapped the layers.

The lantern flame glinted off the dark, mottled sheen of the metal within. A misshapen piece of earthen steel.

Boranson's eyes widened. For the first time, his tired frame seemed to come alive. His chair screeched backward as he surged to his feet, breath caught in his throat. The legs of the chair tipped, and it crashed to the floor, forgotten.

His weathered hands trembled as he pointed at the shard, his voice booming with sudden fury and shock.

"Where did you get that?"

The boy didn't flinch beneath Boranson's anger. His voice came quiet, but steady, calm as still water.

"I got it from my mother," he said. "She told me there would be only one man alive who could recognise the mask of Tareq. That man is you."

Boranson's chest heaved as he stared down at the shard of earthen steel. His gnarled hand twitched, as if ready to seize it from the table, but then he froze. His eyes narrowed.

For the first time, he truly looked at the young man. His gaze slid from the boy's steady eyes down to the cloak draped over his shoulders. There, stitched in silver thread, gleamed the outline of a falcon mid-dive.

Boranson staggered back a half-step, the colour draining from his weathered face. His voice rasped with disbelief.

"...Velmira. You're a Velmira?"

The boy gave the smallest nod. "I am. But I'm not just Velmiran...."

He turned, extending his hand toward the fireplace. The room, once filled with the muted hum of tavern voices, went deathly still. All eyes fixed on him.

The flames within the hearth quivered, then surged. A ribbon of fire tore itself free from the logs, streaming across the open air as if pulled by unseen strings. It coiled around his arm and into his palm, where it bloomed into a sphere of living fire, floating above his hand.

The light of it danced across his face, casting long shadows across the table. He held Boranson's gaze as the flames crackled and spun, steady in his grasp, and gave a wide grin. He held Boranson's gaze without wavering, then let the words fall like hammer strikes.

"My name is Jahlan," he said. "Son of Tsarina Anya Velmira... And Tareq the Flamebearer."

Boranson froze. Falden's hand hovered over the shard on the table, jaw tight. The tavern held its breath.

Jahlan let the flames in his hand gutter and fade until only smoke curled from his fingers. His voice softened, carrying both weight and plea.

"My mother hoped that, if the day ever came, you would remember the bond you once shared. She believed that memory would be enough for you to help those in need now."

He leaned forward across the table, the bundle of cloth with its shard of earthen steel still resting between them.

"My father is gone, and Falden's people need our help. You know how to stand against the darkness. You can stop it. Stand with us as you did before, and help us to turn this tide. If you refuse, countless lives, innocent lives, will die. We need your help, Daran Boranson. The world needs you again."